FINAL PLAY

EDEN FINLEY

FINAL PLAY

To everyone who wasn't ready to let go.
Just like me.

PREMISE

It's a vacation none of them will forget.

Before their futures become the present, Noah convinces his friends they need a group vacation—a final play before they're all tied down by responsibility and unyielding schedules.

Everything is changing.
   Marriage.
   Kids.
   Careers.

A trip to Fiji is the last hurrah to end all hurrahs.

And from disastrous marriage proposals to grand gestures to life-changing confessions, two weeks on a private island becomes the beginning of the rest of their lives.

I
_____

MATT AND NOAH

CHAPTER ONE

MATT

The incessant buzzing of my phone on the bedside table drags me from sleep. I've been avoiding it for about five minutes now, and every time it stops, it picks right back up. It's the middle of the goddamn night.

"I swear if that's Jet drunk dialing us to tell us he misses us again, I'm gonna fly him home to give him a hug and shut him up," Noah grumbles.

"Not if I kill him first." I'm not as loving as my husband when my sleep is interrupted.

I reach blindly for my phone. With my eyes still closed, I hit Answer without looking. "Someone better be dead, in jail, or on fire."

"Matt?" The sweet Southern voice hits my ears, and I bolt up in bed, wide-awake in a millisecond. It's not Char, the only sister I'm still in contact with, but that's all I can tell. It makes me feel like a shit brother for not knowing what my own sisters' voices sound like.

It has to be Daisy. Jet and I decided we'd wait until the other kids were eighteen before getting Char to give them our contact details. Daisy turned eighteen a few months ago, and when we didn't hear from her, I figured she didn't want to talk to us—that she was on team homophobe with Mom and Dad.

"What's wrong, Daisy?" It can't be anything good this time of night.

"It ... it's not Daisy."

"Fern?"

"C-Can you ... Can you come get me?"

My heart pounds erratically. "Where are you?"

"O'Hare." Her voice is so small.

In the middle of the night?

Noah sits up, wrapping his arms around me. "Babe?"

"I'm on my way," I say to Fern and end the call.

Noah reaches over and turns on the bedside light while I scramble to find some clothes in my drawers. A shirt is easy. Pants are a different story.

"Another sibling kicked out for being gay?" Noah asks.

I pause. "Fuck, probably. I didn't ask why she's here."

"She's in Chicago?"

"Flew into O'Hare."

"I'll come with you."

I give Noah a pair of his jeans and keep rummaging for my own. "Do I have anything clean?"

"How would I know?"

"Did you do a load of laundry?"

"Did *you*?"

"Fuck."

Noah finds a shirt and throws it on. "You're the one who decided we shouldn't be spoiled brats and canceled the maid service."

I find some sweats in my bottom drawer. "It didn't make sense to have one in New York for half the year and one in Chicago for the rest of the time."

"We're not getting into this again. We need to go rescue your lesbian sister."

We rush for wallets and jackets, my hands shaking as I wrap a scarf around my neck. I'm flustered and trembling by the time we get to the front door of our penthouse apartment.

Noah pulls me close to him, holding me tight but kissing me softly. It's reassuring and pulls me back from going into full-on freak-out mode. For the second time in four years, one of my siblings has escaped Tennessee and come looking for me.

Noah and I have spoken about it before. I've wanted to move my siblings here with us, but because of flitting between Chicago and New York, being preoccupied during football season, as well as Char's updates that everything is going well with them, we decided they might have a more stable life at home. Admittedly, living with our parents was never *great*, but it's not like they're abusive. Just absent.

That's what I tell myself when I feel guilty about not fighting harder for my brother and sisters—but it's not like I can force myself into my siblings' lives. I have no legal rights as the older brother.

I don't know what being in Chicago could mean for Fern. She's seventeen, will be eighteen in a few months, but I don't know what it means legally. If Mom and Dad kicked her out, do I have to file for custody or does the government not care about that stuff? She could become a ward of the state, and in that case, she might have to return to Tennessee. I don't know how these things work.

We never had to worry about this with Jet because he was nineteen when he came to us.

"Babe," Noah says. "We'll work it out."

I let out a loud breath, and my shoulders relax. It never ceases to amaze me how well Noah knows what I need and when I need it.

It's no secret we rushed into the whole marriage thing, getting hitched after only a few months. Our honeymoon phase was literally still during the newly dating phase, so there was a lot of learning about each other.

Now we move in sync and can sense each other's needs.

Noah holds my hand on the way to our building's parking garage, giving me that little bit of extra comfort, letting me know he's here for me.

"Did I ever tell you how grateful I am to have you as my first husband?"

Noah smiles, his bright white teeth and shiny blue-green eyes making his whole face light up. "Not as much as I've told you I'm so happy I took your virginity."

Even years later, we're still debating this. "Except you didn't." I lean in and give a chaste kiss on his lips. "But we don't have time for this argument."

Noah insists on driving, because I'm in no state to be behind the wheel, but thanks to it being so late at night, we make record time to O'Hare and find Fern outside the domestic terminal.

Long brown hair and the terrified look on her face make it easy to spot her. Char has sent photos over the years, but Fern looks so different in person. Older, maybe. Weighed down with stress.

She sits on a bench near the pickup lane, wrapped up in a thick jacket, scarf, leggings, and boots, but she shivers as if she's still freezing. Chicago winters are a lot harsher than what she's used to.

Noah says he'll stay in the car so we don't get told to move along by airport security, and I can't get to her fast enough. The passenger-side door slams shut behind me, making Fern flinch.

Her brown eyes widen and lock on mine, and I tell myself to slow down as I approach her. She hasn't seen me in over ten years, and here I am rushing her like a crazy man.

"Fern?"

"Matt?" she croaks.

She's out of her seat and in my arms so fast, I don't even have time to take her all in. From head to toe, I want to do a thorough check and make sure there's no injuries, she's been fed well, and she's healthy, but her arms lock around me and hold me tight.

"I didn't know what else to do," Fern rushes to get out. "Char ..." She takes a gasping breath in between her words. "She ... gave me ... your ... number."

"What happened, sweetheart? Why didn't you call me first? I could've come pick you up when you landed."

I wait for the inevitable "They kicked me out" or "I like girls" or any other version of that.

What I get is even more of a shock.

Fern steps back, and her jacket falls open. Her delicate hands support her stomach, rubbing circles over a cute little bump. "This is why I didn't call first."

Oh, shit.

When my gaze flies from her belly to her face again, her eyes become shiny.

I have no idea what to say. "I'm guessing you're not going to tell me you're a lesbian."

Yeah, that's probably not the best thing to blurt out.

CHAPTER TWO

NOAH

Whoa. Even from the car, I can see Matt's sister's baby bump. A knock on my window startles me, and I lower it to talk to the security worker.

"You need to move along unless you're picking someone up or dropping someone off."

I point to Matt and his sister. "We're picking her up." I blast the horn to get Matt's attention.

They both jump, lost in conversation, but when Matt sees the security guy, he takes Fern's small carry-on and leads her over to the car.

Fern barely has time to buckle her seat belt before Matt's turning in his seat to grill her.

"Who is he?"

I reach for him and grip his shoulder hard so he has to face the front. "Mind if I get out of the terminal before interrogating her?" I lock eyes with Matt's sister in the rearview mirror.

She's got big brown eyes like Jet, giving her a permanent

doe-eyed expression, and her long brown hair sits in waves below her shoulders, framing her heart-shaped face.

"I'm Noah, your mannerless brother's husband."

She breaks into a smile. "I'm Fern. Your mannerless husband's knocked-up sister."

"So, is sarcasm a Jackson family trait?" I ask.

"Defense mechanism," Matt and Fern say at the same time.

Yikes. With us living so far away and not having much contact with Matt's family, it's easy to forget the real issues he and his siblings have.

"So who is he?" Matt asks again.

"Let the girl breathe," I say.

Fern leans forward. "I already like him more than you, big brother."

When I glance at Matt out of the corner of my eye, I see his gears turning. He'll do anything for his brothers and sisters, and I know he wishes he could do more.

"Fern will tell us when she's ready," I say.

"Aww, that's sweet," Fern says, "but the story is a boring one. Stupid birth control was stupid. You know, I think the ninety percent effective rate is bullshit."

Her accent is as thick as Matt's when he's pissed off.

"So what brings you here?" Matt asks.

"A delayed connecting flight and a whole lot of swollen ankles."

"Funny," Matt says. "I meant how can we help? How far along are you?"

"Almost six months. I didn't actually know until I was about ten weeks."

I tilt my head to the side like a confused dog. "How could you not know?"

"Well, my periods have always been irreg—"

Matt covers his ears. "Lalalalala."

"I tried to … you know … like"—she coughs—"uh, get rid of it? But in Tennessee you need parental consent if you're under eighteen. Mom and Dad told me I'd made my bed and needed to lie in it. Then came the pro-life lecturing."

"Explains why there's six of us," Matt mumbles. "What about the father?"

"Says he doesn't want to be a dad and he's too young and he has a future if we don't have a kid." Emotion clogs her throat. "I was okay with it. I'd kinda accepted it was my fate, you know? Like Mom, and Char. But last week, I got my early acceptance into the University of Tennessee. I sent in my application the week before I found out about …" She points to her belly. "They're offerin' me a softball scholarship and I'm supposed to start next fall, but *this* …"

Even though she spits anger, I see her hand in the rearview mirror moving over her bump lovingly.

My tongue feels thick. "NFL player, rock star, and softball player with early acceptance into college. Are all Jacksons overachievers?"

Matt ignores my attempt at deflection. "So, you're running away? Is that your answer?"

"I-I need a lawyer and can't afford one. Char said you could help."

Okay, not what I was expecting. Why does she need a lawyer?

"Lawyer?" Matt asks.

I meet Fern's eyes in the rearview mirror again. Just in time for her to say, "An adoption lawyer."

The minute the word adoption falls from her lips, I almost crash the damn car.

"Anything you need," Matt says, but I hear the underlying implication.

Deep breaths, Noah.

"She all settled in?" I ask later when Matt comes to bed. He's been in her room for a long time—much longer than it'd take to set up the guest bed with fresh sheets.

We hadn't changed them since the last time Jet's band played in Chicago and he came for a visit.

Matt strips off his sweats and shirt, and I momentarily get distracted by the way his muscles bunch and contract.

Though I know sex is off the table when he falls into bed on his stomach and lets out a grunt that screams exhaustion.

"What are we going to do?"

Oh, God, we can't talk about this *now*.

"I can think of a few things we could do." My hand runs down his back and to his ass. It's a long shot at a distraction, and I'm surprised when Matt spreads his legs a little wider and lifts his hips.

"Mmm, can you top and do all the work? I've got practice tomorrow, and I wanna be all loose."

"If you're not into it—" I'm not usually one to turn down sex of any kind, but I'm not going to guilt him into it.

"I am. I'm just in my head. I want you to fuck me until I can't think about anything but passing out."

"Oh, baby, you know I'm good at that."

"Fucking me brainless?"

"You're a football player. Aren't you already brainless?" I reach over and massage his ass cheek over his boxer briefs.

Matt hums. "If you keep giving me a massage, call me whatever insult you want."

If I didn't know my husband inside and out, I'd feel bad as I reach for the lube because he's so tight with tension and probably not a hundred percent into it. But I do know him, and a good fucking will help.

During football season, when we have sex, I mostly top him. During the off season, it's the other way around. When Matt is stressed and wants out of his head, wants to forget about football and plays and the Super Bowl, he can't get enough of my cock.

I roll on top of him, straddling his ass and blanketing his back with my body. My mouth leaves light kisses across his shoulders as my hands massage down his sides.

Matt moans, and I have to shush him.

"We have to be quiet. Don't want to scare your innocent sister with all the loud gay sex."

"Pfft, innocent. She's the one who's knocked up."

"Pretty sure that didn't happen by doing it the gay way."

Matt snorts.

I shuffle down a little so I can pull his boxers over the round globes of his ass. I don't pull them all the way down his legs, just enough to give me access.

"Mmm, I love my man's bubble butt."

"Hurry up and show it how much," Matt grumbles.

"Want hard and fast?" I already know the answer, but I won't mind tormenting him for a while. "Want me to barely prep you so that when I'm inside you, you feel like I'm tearing

13

you in two? You want to be so full of me, you'll never want to feel empty again?"

My man groans and lifts his hips, trying to rise to his knees, but I'm still sitting on his legs.

I tsk him. "Patience."

"Fuck you and your patience."

"I love it when you talk dirty."

"Noah," he whines. "I need …" His hands fist into his pillow. "I just *need* …"

"I know, baby."

Matt usually likes the games, drawing it out, and the back-and-forth banter we always have. To get to the name-calling and begging so fast, he must really need it.

So I give him what he wants. I don't even start with one finger—just lube up two and get to work. I tease his rim at first, just until he relaxes enough to let me in.

Tension seeps out of him as I finger his ass and prep him, and Matt's not the only one who's impatient. My dick has worked its way out of the hole in the front of my boxers without me even touching it.

It aches and craves friction. I want to reach for it, but Matt becomes too impatient.

"I don't care if I'm not prepped properly. I need you inside me now."

Instead of listening to him though, I scissor my fingers inside him. With him having practice tomorrow, it's important he's not walking funny in the morning.

Matt turns into a quivering mess, moaning into his pillow and pushing his ass as high as he can get it. He clenches around my fingers, greedy for more.

I don't bother taking off my boxers. Instead, I cover my

exposed cock with lube, hold Matt's ass cheeks apart, and dive right in.

Asking Matt to be quiet on a good day is hard enough, but the shout of pure pleasure as I enter him shouldn't be heard outside this room. The Chicago apartment seems more sound-proof than the town house in New York. Even if she can hear it, with how keyed up we are, I know the noises won't last for long.

I take a deep breath and will myself not to come inside Matt's tight ass yet. I need to take a moment, no matter how many impatient noises my husband makes to get me to move.

"Need you," Matt whispers.

"I've got you." I pull back, dragging my cock slowly out until only the tip remains. I flatten my chest against his back.

I thrust inside hard, and Matt shudders. Starting at a slow pace, I move in and out of him until I can't take it slow anymore.

I grip his hips and pull myself upright.

"Yes," he hisses.

I take Matt hard and fast, and it doesn't take long for sweat to drip down my chest, my muscles to tire, and my balls to ache.

Matt tenses and grunts through his orgasm, his tight ass contracting around my cock and milking it.

After he melts into the mattress and I come down from the high, I pull out of him, kiss his shoulder, and flop onto the bed beside him.

"Love you," I say.

"Yeah, you do."

I laugh, because I'm usually the one to mouth off at affection.

"Love you too," he adds.

I don't know what's going to happen with Matt's sister, what it means for Matt's and my relationship, but I do know I'll do anything for my man.

Even if it scares the shit out of me. Because there's no doubt in my mind what's going on in my husband's brain.

CHAPTER THREE

MATT

Noah's trying to hide that he's freaking out, and if I'm honest, I know exactly how he feels. I want to do everything I can to help Fern. In what capacity, I'm not sure yet—whatever she needs. But I saw the second she mentioned an adoption lawyer, Noah's panic began. Because he knows me. He knows I'd want to protect my niece or nephew any way I could even if it means looking after them myself if it came down to it.

Yeah, she could adopt the kid out to strangers through an agency, but what if they get parents worse than ours? I don't want to even think about it. Noah and I have the money and ability to take care of a child.

I think Noah would make a great dad, but the topic of kids is something we've never discussed. It's another pitfall to rushing into marriage. We hadn't had time to discuss it before we got hitched. I have always figured if I'm going to do the kid thing, I'll do it after I retire from the NFL. It's always been a future issue and one I haven't had to think about seriously.

But the future problem is here now, and I'm not surprised to wake up to an empty bed. Noah waking before me can only mean one thing. He didn't sleep much, if at all.

I get up and shower, because I'll be no good to anyone before I feel human, and after I get dressed and make my way into the kitchen, I find Noah unpacking breakfast from the café downstairs in our apartment building.

"Morning," I say and kiss his cheek as if nothing's wrong.

That's something that hasn't changed. We're still great at distraction, miscommunicating, and pretending everything is okay. We've just learned to handle the fallout of it better.

"Pregnant people eat lots, don't they?" Noah asks.

I take in the amount of food he's bought. "Yeah, but I think you've mistaken being pregnant with being the Warriors' entire defensive line."

Noah shrugs. "We'll eat leftovers."

He moves around the kitchen, avoiding eye contact with me.

"Noah—"

I'm taken off guard and stumble back when his arms come around me and his face burrows into my neck. "I'll do it. I know you'll want to help Fern and her baby, and I'll do whatever you're planning, because I agreed when I married you to support you."

I hold him tight because he's tense as fuck, but his words confuse me, because I haven't actually said my plans out loud. "Wait, wait, wait. Back up. What are you actually saying here? Is this why you didn't sleep last night?"

"Fern wants to meet with an adoption lawyer, you want to help Fern. I can already see where this is going, Matt. I didn't want to face it last night, but I'm ready."

"We should sit down and discuss it properly."

Noah shakes his head. "I don't need to. I love you. You're my forever. And I spent all night telling myself that even if I'm scared fucking shitless and would make a terrible role model for a child—"

"You're great with Jet when he's home. You've been great with him ever since he came to us."

"He was nineteen. That doesn't count. I know nothing about babies or little kids."

"Neither do most first-time parents."

Noah backs up until he's leaning against the kitchen counter. "First-time … par …"

"Breathe, hon."

He shakes off his panic and stands taller. Totally faking it, but I love him for trying.

"I can do this," he says. "Even though I'm terrified, it's nowhere near as terrifying as risking you. I'm with you, babe. Wherever this takes us."

I smile. "That'd be so much more convincing if you weren't freaking out right now."

"I'll stop soon. I promise."

One obstacle taken care of. Sort of. Knowing Noah's with me eases any doubt or worry of how we're going to tackle Fern's situation. Which, we still don't know much about, so this conversation could all be for nothing.

"For the record"—I pull Noah closer so he's pressed against me again—"I think you'd make an excellent father."

"Not as good as you would. You practically raised all your siblings. You've already been a dad figure."

I go to open my mouth, but he cuts me off.

"If you make a Daddy joke right now, I'll punch you."

19

I laugh. "I'm going to try to find a lawyer today after practice."

"I can do that. You focus on football."

"After we meet with a lawyer, we'll know more. Try not to stress about it, okay?"

"Okay."

I know that's easier said than done, because if Fern does put her baby up for adoption, there's a very real chance we could become parents.

Kids may not have been on my radar, but with one pregnant belly, I realize it's something I want.

And speaking of pregnant bellies, Fern and hers appear. "Mornin'."

She's wearing what we picked her up in: boots, leggings, short skirt, black tank top, and a gray cardigan, sans her thick jacket. She had a small bag with her, but I'm guessing she didn't bring many clothes.

"Good morning," I say.

"Coffee?" Noah asks.

I backhand his stomach. "Pregnant."

"So?"

"I'm not supposed to have caffeine," Fern says.

"No coffee? Like you're not being tortured enough." Noah winces, realizing comments like that probably don't help her situation.

But Fern doesn't seem to care. "I'm not much of a coffee drinker anyway. Thank you though."

"Hungry? Noah bought enough to feed you for days, possibly weeks."

My husband gives me the finger. He really loves me.

"Yes. Food. Food good," Fern says. "I don't think I've eaten so much in my life."

"Growing body parts is hard, I imagine," I say.

Fern screws up her face. "It sounds gross when you put it that way."

"Yeah, it really does," Noah agrees.

As we sit down to eat at the dining table, I get straight to business. We didn't get a chance to talk much last night because it was so late, but now I need to know everything.

"How long are you here for?" I ask.

"I don't know? Long enough to talk to a lawyer and figure out my options, I guess. I mean, if that's okay with you. If you'll help. I know I have no right to—"

"Fern. It's okay. I'm here for you no matter what. Actually, that's something we should talk about ..."

"I know about the trusts you set up in our names." Brown eyes blink at me.

"Char?"

She shakes her head. "Daisy."

"But Daisy didn't take it. Or contact me. Or—"

"She's dating someone from a super-rich, super-conservative family. So ..."

"So, she's team Mom and Dad." I eye her, trying to gauge her opinion of it. Maybe she feels the same but is desperate for money. Not that I wouldn't give it to her if she didn't "approve of my lifestyle" and all that other bullshit. Like Noah said, I practically raised my siblings, and while it breaks my heart that Daisy would choose our parents and their stupid views over me, I can't help feeling responsible for them still.

I should maybe see a therapist about that, but whatever.

"What about you?" I ask. "Do you agree with Daisy or Char?"

She cocks her head. "Don't worry, brother. If I agreed with Daisy, I never would've come here. From what I can tell, Daisy's the only one who got that gene."

"How's Wade?"

The smile that takes over her face makes me think of her when she was little. It makes my chest ache.

"Wade is the smartest of us all. He's in all these advanced classes. He's gonna be like a scientist or some shit. Maybe a doctor. Although, blood makes him squirm, so I don't think he'll be a good one."

"Really?" Genuine pride fills my veins. "That's so awesome. Is he happy? Did we ..." Did we make the right decision leaving them in Tennessee?

"Did you what?"

Noah holds my hand and answers for me. "We've been wondering if we should've fought for you guys. Back when Jet turned up on our doorstep, we asked ourselves if we should try to move all of you here. But—"

"It wasn't your job to raise us. Or take care of us."

Tears spring to my eyes. "I've always felt guilty. Like I should be doing more than sending money."

Fern huffs. "You went through enough at home. I know that. I might not know exactly what, but gay guys in our town don't exist. The ones who are don't stick around, and it's easy to see why. You don't owe us anything. If it weren't for this baby, I wouldn't want my trust. Not because it comes from you, but because I want my achievements to be mine. Like my softball scholarship. You taught us all to make our own way by

22

not even being there, and you shouldn't feel guilty about getting yourself out of a shitty situation."

It's exactly what I need to hear.

"And Wade ... he's doing so well. I wouldn't want to disturb that. But if you've got money for an Ivy League for him in a few years, I'm sure he'll be grateful. Though I suspect he'll have scholarship offers up the wazoo."

"I'm so proud of you. Both you and Wade."

She stares down at her pregnant belly. "Because I clearly make awesome choices?"

"You got a sports scholarship, Fern. That's amazing. Even if you can't accept it. You earned it."

"I *want* to accept it. But I want a lot of things that aren't possible."

Noah downs the rest of his coffee. "I'm gonna go ... uh ... run some errands."

"If I don't see you before I leave for practice, have a good day," I say, and he comes to kiss my cheek before heading for the door.

I hold my breath as I watch Noah leave. He should be here for this discussion, but maybe it's too much.

Maybe it's too much for me to ask this of him. He says he's with me, but is he really? Or does he just know he has to deal with it because he knows I'm going to help my family no matter what?

Our group of friends doesn't really understand my relationship with my family back in Tennessee. I don't know if Noah or Jet told them or if they guessed that I'm financially supporting my homophobic parents. It doesn't help that Jet said goodbye to them and that life the minute he stepped onto a Greyhound bus.

What they don't understand is, it's not my folks I'm supporting but the kids I helped raised. I'd do anything for my siblings, even Daisy if she asked for it. Unconditional love is like that.

I reach for Fern's hands, but she doesn't lift her head.

"What's wrong?" I place a finger under her chin and force her to look at me.

Her cheeks are wet with tears. "Everything?" She sniffs. "I had a plan. Fuckface and I had a plan!"

I huff a laugh. "Does fuckface have a name, or will he forever be fuckface?"

"Darryl. But fuckface works."

"So, what was your plan?"

"I was going to go to college while he stayed home with the kid and worked nights."

"That sounds like a hectic schedule for a seventeen-year-old."

"I'm not dumb enough to think it'd be easy, but I don't think it's the money thing or the workload. I think his parents got in his head about it being the mother's job to stay at home or some bullshit, because suddenly it's like being a stay-at-home father is a threat to his masculinity or something."

"Maybe it's that you're teenagers and he's freaking out. Maybe he just needs time?"

"I don't know, but something scared him off. If he was in college, then yeah, I could stay with the kid while he went to school. But he's not. He dropped out of high school and is working a dead-end, minimum-wage job, and I want a proper future. There's no way I can work to pay the bills, study, and look after a kid. I don't want to be like our parents, but it's hard when we can't even get a start, you know?"

"I'm happy to take you to an adoption lawyer so you can

work out your options, but before we do all that, are you sure this is what you want?"

In one conversation, I already know what Fern wants. It's obvious. She wants her future, but she also already loves the child inside her so much.

I'm more than willing to give her the money for a lawyer, but I think it'll be a waste of time.

She confirms my suspicions when she rubs a hand over her stomach. "I want everything. Is that so much to ask?"

I laugh. "No, it's not. And I'm gonna give it to you."

CHAPTER FOUR

NOAH

I probably should stay for their conversation, but I don't want to let my headspace show. I'm not one hundred percent sure I could be in the same room as Fern without having a panic attack, and I doubt she'll want to give her baby to a guy who's breaking out in hives over the idea of being a dad.

Because I *know* that's how this is going to end.

I wander around aimlessly before making my way across to Millennium Park and sit by the water even if it's below freezing out here.

Googling family lawyers in Chicago and calling to make an appointment with one only makes it more real, but I do it anyway.

With an appointment booked for tomorrow and Matt leaving for practice soon, I should go back to the apartment and face this like an adult.

Instead, I sit in the cold with frost on the ground, the wind blowing, my face stinging, and I tell myself to suck it up.

Maybe I should think about it in terms of if I were straight and some pregnant chick turned up saying it's my baby.

That lasts about three minutes before I give up because it's just not plausible enough to wrap my head around.

When that fails, I take out my phone again and Skype call Aron and Wyatt in New York. Out of everyone I know, they're the ones to talk to about this.

The screen comes to life, and all I can see are the big chubby cheeks and pouty lips of baby Ryan.

"Yeah, yeah, your baby's cute, but I need to talk to an adult."

Aron pulls his phone back so I can see his face and baby Ryan normal-sized. Shit, not so much *baby* Ryan anymore. Toddler Ryan? Is there an in-between from baby to toddler? That's what Ryan is.

Oh yeah, I could be a fucking parent. I don't even know kid stages.

Aron and Wyatt went from friends to lovers to big happy family so ridiculously fast, but I can't be happier for them. And even though they've been together as long as Matt and I have, it's hard to remember a time where they *weren't* together. I could swear they were together way back in college even though they weren't. It's as if they've always come as a package.

"Is that your motto in life?" Aron asks. "I need an actual adult, because I don't think I'm equipped to deal with what-ever life is throwing at me?"

I scowl. Aron laughs.

Wyatt's blond head leans over Aron's shoulder. "Hi, Noah. Bye, Noah. I gotta get to work."

They give each other a peck on the lips, Wyatt kisses the

top of Ryan's head, and then he disappears from the screen again.

"So, what's up?" Aron asks.

"How's fatherhood?" My tone's forced casualness goes unnoticed.

"Fucking tiring. Ryan's teething, so he's fussy all the time and whiny and clingy, and Wyatt gets home from work and riles him all up, and then it takes *forever* for him to get to sleep, and then—" He stops abruptly. "Wait. You never ask about Ryan or fatherhood. You say he's cute and then change the subject whenever we bring him up." He assesses me through the screen, but he's not going to get anything from me. My eyes are probably bloodshot from the wind, and I'm keeping my face as neutral as possible. "Are you ... Does Matt ... Are you guys talking about kids? Is that the reason why you're sitting on a park bench in the freezing cold?"

"How'd you know I was in a park? You can only see my face."

"You look like you're about to turn into a Popsicle. I guessed. So spill it."

"Matt's talking about kids. Well, kid. His sister's kid. She wants to put it up for adoption, and I know Matt will want to take in the kidlet."

"Without discussing it with you first?"

"Oh, he will, but how am I supposed to say, 'No, you can't provide a stable life for your blood niece or nephew, because I'm a selfish, selfish man.'"

"Well, you are that," Aron says dryly, then turns serious. "Just talk to him. Tell him you're not ready."

"How did you know you were ready?"

"Wyatt and I *talked* about it. Together." Aron gasps. "Shocking concept for you and Matt, I know."

"Hey, we talk. I kind of already told him I'm in this with him whatever he wants."

Aron chuckles. "Of course you did. So, your choices are either go back home and say, 'No, wait, let's talk about this before I make any impulsive decisions' or you need to come to terms with adopting an actual real-life human baby in a few months. How far along is she?"

"Umm ... I don't know, but you can tell she's pregnant just by looking at her."

"Okay, so you need to come to terms with it super fast. When we were looking into options, adoption was going to take a few years, and when Rebecca and Skylar offered, we still had the whole pregnancy to get used to it. You don't have that luxury."

Nope. Certainly don't.

"For what it's worth? As exhausted as I am, I wouldn't trade Ryan for the world. He and Wyatt are my everything."

And Matt's my everything. I'll move heaven and earth for him, and that sounds a lot harder than simply having a baby.

Right?

When I do eventually come home at dinnertime, my brave face is in place.

"Hey, you're home," Matt says.

"Yeah, sorry I was gone all day. I ended up at the new Rainbow Beds."

29

After I hung up from Aron, I decided to actually be productive for the day.

Matt smiles at me. Rainbow Beds in New York was my baby, but I gave up the reins three years ago when it kept pulling my attention away from Matt in Chicago during football season. I'm still involved but not in charge, and a Chicago location is opening soon, so I'm pitching in where I can.

It worked for a great distraction today.

"I managed to get an appointment for tomorrow for the lawyer," I say.

Matt's face falls a little. "Thanks, but I should've messaged. We, uh"—he glances at his sister and then back at me—"don't need it anymore."

My brow furrows.

"I'm keeping the baby," Fern says.

This is the part where I'm supposed to be overjoyed. Ecstatic. Feel like I'm free of all responsibility, because let's face it, I think I'm allergic to that.

But I'm not any of those things.

Surprising disappointment kicks me in the nuts. I was so sure I knew where this was heading—me, Matt, and a baby.

I spent all day getting used to the idea. I should be relieved. Why am I not relieved? Not even a little bit?

Sitting through dinner, I keep telling myself what no baby means.

Nothing changes.

I love my life.

There's no longer the threat of a screaming baby and diapers filling my future.

I can day drink!

Okay, yeah, I don't do that. But I could take it up.

As Jet would say, *hashtag life goals.*

"I'm exhausted," I say.

"Conveniently too exhausted to do the dishes?" Matt asks.

"Of course." I stand and head for our bedroom, singing, "Shouldn't have fired the maid."

Fern laughs.

I strip down and get into bed, still unable to shake the disappointment.

Matt comes in after he cleans up after dinner.

His arms wrap around me as he climbs into bed and rolls me over to face him. "She never wanted to give the baby up. She just thought she had no other option."

"So what did you give her?" I ask.

"Money." He stops me before I can interrupt. "I know what you're thinking—what if she's like our parents and won't stop, but we made a deal. I'm paying for her living and childcare expenses so she can go to school and not have to worry about getting a job. Raising a baby while studying is gonna be hard enough without student loan debt or bills to worry about. She's smart. She wants to stay and work in Tennessee when she graduates, and I'm giving her the chance to pay me back— those were her terms. You should've seen her face when I gave her the option of having both school and the baby."

I can tell he's disappointed even if he's happy for his sister. "You're sad though."

Matt shakes his head. "Nah. I'm happy it's just you and me. A screaming baby? No, thanks." He's about as convincing as one of my dad's old political promises.

"Can I admit something to you?"

"Always. But let me guess. You're relieved as fuck."

I take a deep breath, because admitting this is hard, and I

know once this is out there, it's gonna change everything. "I'm disappointed."

"What?"

"I had less than twenty-four hours to get used to the idea, but I did. I've been freaking out all day, but the second you said we don't need the lawyer anymore, it was as if you'd stolen something from me. I was convinced it was going to happen, so I made myself come to terms with it. Now that it's not? I think ... I mean ... I really fucking want it. I'm not going to go psycho on your sister and try to steal her baby, but ... I want to have kids with you. Wait, maybe kid. Let's start with one and see where we go from there."

Matt's face lights up. I can't imagine a world where he doesn't have that smile on his face, and I don't want to.

"It doesn't have to be now or soon or whatever, but yeah ... I want a kid with you."

"Are you serious right now?" It makes sense he doesn't believe me.

"As a heart attack."

"Did you just compare being a parent to having a heart attack?"

"Yup."

The revelation hangs in the air.

"Holy shit," Matt whispers.

"Do you think if I fuck you hard enough, I could get you pregnant?"

Matt breaks into a booming laugh, but in the next second, he's on top of me and I'm pinned on my back. "I'm willing to try, though it'd totally be the other way around."

I shrug. "I say we try as much as possible, every which way. We will break the laws of biology, damn it."

"Sounds like a plan."

"We better contact an adoption agency though too. You know, just in case."

"That sounds like a better plan. Less fun, but probably more effective."

"Probably. Aron said the wait list was years. If we do it now, maybe I'll be definitely ready by the time we get a baby."

"You spoke to Aron today?"

I nod. "He told me parenthood is so exhausting and the kid's a brat, but as soon as he found out about your pregnant sister, he was all 'oh, parenting is the best thing ever.' I feel like it's a trap. But it was a convincing one. I want a family with you one day."

"I want that too."

CHAPTER FIVE

MATT

Thirty thousand feet in the air, somewhere over Kentucky, the reality of going home finally hits. I haven't been back to Tennessee in ten years unless it's been for a game, and if any of my family was at those games, I wouldn't know. I've had no desire to step back into that toxic environment. Still don't.

But Fern is giving birth to my nephew, and she's asked me to be there, so I'm freaking doing it even if it means seeing the rest of my family who I haven't spoken to since I was outed four years ago.

Noah's hand lands on my bouncing leg, stilling it. "Stop."

"Sorry."

"You mind joining the pilot in the cockpit?" he asks his flight attendant.

She gives a knowing nod. "We're landing in thirty minutes." That's all she says before she leaves us in the main cabin.

Noah unclicks his seat belt. "Plenty of time." He sinks to his knees in front of me, but I put my hand on his shoulder.

"Thanks, but I don't think my head's in it."

"That's the point. You need to relax. And don't worry, more than just your head can fit in my mouth." He winks.

There's really no point in trying to stop him, plus my dick is already on board even if I'm not in the mood.

"Remember the first time we ever hooked up?" Noah says while unzipping my fly. "It was right here, in this very spot."

"Technically, it was over the Atlantic Ocean." My mouth is dry, my voice gruff.

"If we want to get technical." Noah frees me from my jeans. "You were such a grumpy asshole."

"You were an entitled bastard."

"I'm still that." Noah lowers his head, licking the tip of my cock.

I suck in a sharp breath. "And I can still be a grumpy asshole."

"Not if I'm choking on your dick." He takes me into his wet heat and sucks me all the way to the root.

"I love your mouth."

"Mmhmm," he hums, sending vibrations down to my toes.

"I love *you*," I chant. "Love you, love you, love you."

Noah pulls off with a wet pop. "That's more like it." He sucks a finger into his mouth, and I know what's coming.

"Fuck yes." I work my pants down my thighs farther and move my ass to the edge of my seat.

When Noah's mouth goes back to my cock, his finger teases the rim of my ass and slowly pushes inside.

"More," I demand.

He does as I ask without cracking a joke like he normally

EDEN FINLEY

would, and not for the first time in the years we've been married I'm thankful when Noah knows when I need him to just give instead of continuing the normal push and pull between us.

While Noah fingers my ass, he sucks on my dick like he's getting paid for it. Warm saliva coats my cock, while two of his fingers rub against my prostate.

I warn him with plenty of time for him to move out of the way, but he doesn't. I come on a hoarse cry, and he swallows it all—something he only does when he feels like being nice. Which is rarely, because he's Noah.

He pulls back and wipes his mouth. "Less messy." He grins.

I reach for his fly when he stands. "Your turn."

His hand covers mine to stop me. "That was for you, because I know you needed it."

Leaning in, he kisses me with the same amount of passion he's always had for me, and all the good feelings from the amazing blowjob float away with the notion that I'm walking my man—the love of my life—into a lion's den.

Noah and I have been through some hard times, but introducing my black husband to my homophobic, racist parents? Fern owes me, and I mean more than money.

I don't want to put Noah through their judgment and scrutiny. He deserves better than that. They may be my family by blood, but Noah is my *world*.

Noah takes his seat again and wraps his arm around me. As if sensing what I'm worried about, he says, "I'm here, babe. No matter what they throw at us."

I lean into him and take deep calming breaths, trying to prepare myself for seeing my family again.

When we land, Char's there to meet us in the private charter lounge.

At least we're starting off with the nice family member and someone Noah's met before. She hugs us both, which surprises Noah.

"Where's your gaggle of children?" I ask.

"At home with their daddy. He called it *babysitting*. Can you believe that? He deserves to be left alone with them. Until he learns to call looking after his kids *parenting*, he's gonna be doin' as much 'babysittin'' as he can."

I have to admit her baby daddy is a bit of a stereotypical small-town Southern man. Bless his heart. I paid for Char, her partner, and their two kids to come to New York two years ago during the off-season. He hated every second of being in "the big, noisy city." He was surprisingly supportive of Noah and me though. Maybe it's because he knows if it weren't for us, they'd still be living in a trailer.

My sister is content to be a Stuart Crossing stay-at-home mom, and that's her prerogative. Since then, she's popped out another kidlet I haven't met, and three kids in four years is an amazing feat. She says she's gonna prove she's a better mom than our own. That seems to be her only goal in life. And hell, I understand it.

If … no—*when*—Noah and I get our baby, it's going to be my number one priority to let him or her know they're loved no matter who they grow up to be. I'm going to support them, discipline them, but most of all, I'm going to love them. I will be there for them through everything—not pick and choose when and under what circumstances.

Whenever they come to us.

We've been with our adoption agency for a few months,

which is no time at all in adoption land, but they said with us being a high-profile couple and in the media, we'll most likely have more people interested in giving us their child.

Was it weird hearing that? Absolutely.

But it seems like it might not have been true, because we haven't been picked yet.

It's still early, I remind myself. *Adoption takes years.*

It's funny that we went from not even discussing it to wanting it so badly this quickly, but Noah and I are the same in the way that when we decide we want something, we go for it. Once our mind is made up, there's no changing it.

Though, I think I'm the only one super eager for it. Noah's still in the mindset it'll take years, so he's taking this time to mentally prepare himself.

"How's Fern doing?" I ask as we make our way out to Char's car.

"She's hanging in there."

"She's still in labor?" Noah exclaims. "She called us, like, twelve hours ago."

"Yup. Our nephew is stubborn." Char cocks her head. "I wonder where he gets that from?"

"Clearly from Aunt Char," I say.

"Mmhmm."

Char catches us up on the latest happenings in my siblings' lives, including the news that Daisy's engaged to the conservative trust fund kid. Wade is still doing well at school, and Fern's all set to move to Knoxville once she graduates high school in a couple of months.

"I should warn you …" Char says as we pull into the parking lot of the hospital. "Mom and Dad are here."

I figured as much, but I had hoped they wouldn't bother. "Good plan telling me with no time to prepare to see them."

Noah squeezes my shoulder from the back seat. "It's fine. We can handle it."

"Do they know what I did for Fern?" I stare out the windshield at a building that's not supposed to be intimidating but suddenly is.

"They do," Char says. "I think they have some kind of loophole in their bigotry."

I nod. "Right. As long as the money keeps coming, they can ignore me and pretend they don't need me."

"Can I ask you something?" Char's voice is small.

"Anything."

"Why do you still give them money?"

Noah and I have had this exact same conversation, and the truth is, I don't know anymore. The excuse I'd used the past few years is they had Daisy, Fern, and Wade, and I didn't want my siblings to suffer or miss out. But now Wade is the only one left, and in three years, he'll be out of the house too. I don't know what my move will be then.

They're my parents. They gave me life. Dad gave me my love of football and spared no expense when I was a kid to make sure I had the right opportunities open to me.

No, he wasn't a great father. Yes, he caused me to have internalized homophobia for a long time before I dealt with it. And yes, he now treats me and Jet like pariahs. But where's the line?

When you owe your family everything, how much money does it cost to repay your debt?

Noah found it easy to write off his cold father, but there's a difference between my dad and his. When faced with the possibility of losing Noah, his father wanted to make the effort to fix their broken relationship. Mine is the one who shut me out.

"Maybe I'll rethink it once Wade is in college," I mutter.

Char pats my arm. "If I don't tell you enough, you're the best big brother we could've asked for, and if the others don't tell you, we all appreciate you. Even Daisy, who doesn't actually know how much you've done for her by keeping Mom and Dad afloat these past few years."

I chew my bottom lip. "Dad still gambling?"

Char mirrors my nervous habit. "I don't ... I'm not ..."

"You don't know if he is or not?"

"Oh, I know the answer. I just don't want to tell you."

I throw my head back on the headrest of my seat. "That bad?"

"They take your money for granted, and it pisses me the fuck off. I have no doubt in my mind that I'd still be livin' in a trailer if it weren't for you, and I'm not going to take advantage of that like they do. There's a difference between getting a leg up and extortion. Don't help them, Matt. I'm beggin' you to step away so they can be the grown-ups they're supposed to be for once. If they ask for money, say no. *Please*."

"And what about Wade?"

"Don't you get it? They ain't givin' Wade any of your money. They're wastin' it."

"What am I supposed to do, then?"

Suddenly, my sister looks sheepish. "You know how we promised not to tell Wade anything until he turned eighteen like the others? Well, I kinda, sorta ... after the whole Fern thing where she got to find out earlier than planned, I thought Wade—"

40

"We did that for a reason. Wade is still a minor. If Mom and Dad don't want me anywhere near him, they can legally make me stay away."

"Look, I know this trip is about Fern and her baby, but I've been thinking ..."

"What?"

"Wade is so smart. He really has the brains to do more than all of us. Who knows where he gets it from, but could you imagine what he could do if he went to one of the top schools in the country? In, say, New York or Chicago?"

It suddenly clicks. "You want me to take Wade."

She bites her lip again. "Actually, Fern and I both think it's what would be best for Wade."

"What does Wade think?"

"We haven't discussed it with him. We wanted to talk to you first."

I sigh. "I should've fought harder for y'all."

"Don't make me slap you," Char says. "Up until this year, everything has been fine, I swear it. It's just Wade is something special, you know? Taking him full-time is a big ask, and you have no responsibility toward him, but ... we all want what's best for him. There's no contest between you and our parents. You can give him the future he deserves."

"And if he don't wanna come with me? If he turns out to be like Daisy and rejects my help?"

"Then maybe he ain't as smart as his IQ suggests."

Noah's quiet in the back, which can't be a good sign. He surely has opinions on this even if he's always said he'll go along with whatever I decide because they're my family.

Char's phone pings. "Baby Nat is here," she singsongs.

"Saved by the bell," Noah murmurs.

Oh, yeah, he has opinions.

That'll be fun later.

I open my car door. "Baby time."

You're doing this for your nephew. You can do it.

"What in the ever-lovin' fuck you doin' here?" My father's voice booms across the waiting room.

A few people turn their heads.

Way to stay inconspicuous.

Whether they don't recognize me or they're preoccupied with being in a hospital for whatever reason, they all go back to their own business while we approach my dad.

I mumble to Char, "I'm guessin' while you didn't tell me Mom and Dad would be here, you didn't tell them neither."

I'm starting to think my sister should keep her ridiculous sheepish look on her face for the rest of our trip. It'll save time.

"Worst. Sister. Ever."

Even at fifty-two, my father's still stocky and domineering. I take after him with my height and physique. Jet takes after Mom. Dad's salt-and-pepper hair is new. He always said I'd make him go gray. Apparently not seeing me for almost ten years did it.

Noah squeezes my hand, which only makes my father's gaze dart toward our intertwined fingers.

"I was invited," I say, my voice gruff. "Where's Mom?"

My dad ignores me.

A guy stands from one of the chairs and moves next to Dad. It takes a second for me to register that it's not some random guy. It's my baby brother. Fifteen years old and taller than both Dad and me.

He folds his lanky arms across a slim chest, and it seems he takes after Dad's height but Mom's thin frame. He has Jet's wispy, shaggy hair and the Jackson trademark brown eyes.

"Wade" falls from my mouth.

His stern face falters a tiny bit, but he stays strong.

"You're not welcome here," Dad says again. He glances at Noah. "Neither of you are."

"Dad," Char says. "Fern wanted him here."

"I'm the one payin' for Fern's apartment, education, and for that baby," I say. "You expect me to stay away because you don't want me? Fern wants me here, and you cain't do nothin' 'bout it."

Damn my Southern accent. At least my family won't know something's up and I'm barely holding it together, because they've only known me with my accent. With the way Noah holds on to my hand tighter though, he knows exactly how close I am to losing it.

"I told you when you were eighteen not to bother comin' back."

"And the only reason I listened was because I didn't want to drag the kids into our mess."

Wade's brow scrunches, and he looks at Dad, but Dad's too busy scowling at me to notice.

"We just want to see the baby, and then we'll be on our way," I say.

"Matt?" Mom's quiet voice makes us all turn toward the doors leading to the maternity suite.

I meet eyes with the woman who gave birth to me. The person who didn't protect her son from her husband's toxic views and even encouraged negativity. And as Dad takes her arm and charges past us to move toward the exit, I realize that hasn't changed.

They haven't changed. They never will. I don't know why I was holding on to the possibility of things being different.

Maybe that's why I've been supporting them all these years.

They say blood is thicker than water, but I read somewhere once that maple syrup is thicker than blood. Therefore, pancakes are more important than family.

I thought it was a joke until this very minute when I watch my parents walk out.

They will always walk out on me, so why the fuck am I trying to hold on to that?

"Wade," my father barks.

Wade glances between me and our parents before his feet shuffle after them.

I sidestep to cut him off. "If you want to know the truth about what's happened in the last ten years, we're staying at the Omni Hotel."

"He's not interested," Dad answers.

"Thanks for answering, *Wade*."

Wade looks torn but follows our parents out.

"Who doesn't love family reunions?" I say sarcastically.

Noah puts his arm around me. "I'm sorry, baby."

"I'm sorry too," Char says.

"It actually wasn't as bad as I expected. Let's go get nephew cuddles."

I'm able to play off my encounter with my family, but I'd be lying if I said I wasn't dying on the inside.

CHAPTER SIX

NOAH

My man is struggling. He covers it well for his sisters, but he can't hide it from me.

"So what's with the name Nat?" Matt asks as he looks adoringly at his newborn nephew. I think Nat's supporting Matt more than the other way around.

Fern smiles. "I named him after his uncles. Noah and Matt. Nat."

Matt almost drops the damn baby.

Yeah, we're going to make great parents.

"You … name … baby … me." Matt scrambling for words is adorable.

"What he's trying to say is we're honored," I supply for him.

Matt nods. "Yeah. That."

The way he sways, holding the little blue bundle in his arms, it unlocks another part of my heart I didn't even know was closed up.

I see our future and want it more now than ever.

Am I completely shitting myself over being a father? More so than anything I've ever freaked out over before. But I figure if anyone could be good parents, it'd be me and Matt. We'd know what *not* to do.

Although, surprisingly, my father has never been more pleasant to deal with. After he had the rude awakening that the rest of the country didn't buy his bullshit and Mom convinced him to finally give up the White House, we actually get along now. Matt and I have meals with my parents whenever we're in New York.

It's *weird.*

Standing up to my father changed our entire relationship, and when he realized he had absolutely no control over me, he stopped trying.

If anyone had told me a few years ago that I'd be the one with the more stable family environment, I would've laughed in their face.

But I'd trade my somewhat healthier relationship with my parents for Matt's family to accept him in a heartbeat. I can handle my cold-hearted father and lukewarm mother. Matt can't handle his family's rejection.

I wish I could take away that pain for him, but short of yelling at him that his family will never change—which is just plain mean—I don't know what I can do to help him.

Helplessness isn't a new emotion for me, but it's never hurt this bad.

Matt hands the baby back and kisses Fern on the forehead as we leave.

Char drops us at the hotel, and Matt's quiet the entire ride and for check-in.

Not even naming rights over baby Nat is enough for him to forget the interaction with his parents and brother.

It's not until we reach the room that he finally lets go. He collapses on the bed and curls into a ball.

I hate seeing him this way. Hate it. It makes me want to hurt his parents. Okay ... I'd totally hire someone to do it. I can't get my hands dirty. But it makes me hate them even more than I already do.

Climbing on the bed next to Matt, I sit against the head-board and put his head in my lap. I run my fingers through his hair and ignore the tears on his cheeks. Some shit from his childhood he still can't shake—like not wanting to show emotion to anyone—so I don't call him on it or draw attention to it.

We stay like that for God knows how long.

I want to fix him, comfort him, and wrap him in a bubble so no one would ever hurt him.

Matt's breathing evens out, and I think he's asleep, but when the phone starts ringing in the room, he sits up in a rush with his face scrunched in confusion.

"It's okay," I say to him. "It's the front desk. Lie back down."

But he doesn't. He reaches for the phone, and the hope he had earlier today is back. He just spent who knows how long crying himself to sleep, and now it's like this afternoon never happened.

I wish he didn't care so much. It's so much easier not to get hurt when you have zero expectations. It's armor I've used my entire life. It's how I've survived. Which is why I have no idea how to help Matt.

Matt answers the phone and mutters a few *okays* and *uh-huhs* into it.

When he hangs up, I look at him expectantly.

"My mom and brother are in the lobby. They're coming up now."

And the cycle continues. I force a smile but prepare to tell those fuckers to leave if I need to.

"They wouldn't have come if they didn't care," I lie. They could be here to tell him to leave town again for all I know.

There's a light rap on the door, and Matt takes a deep breath.

"I'll get it." Maybe I can tell them to fuck off before they say it to him, but of course, Matt follows me all the way to the door, and I feel him at my back as I swing it open to greet them.

Matt's mother, Jennifer, is nothing like I'd imagined her to be. Earlier in the hospital, she appeared demure. Quiet. I guess I was expecting a white-trash loudmouth. Not this woman in front of me—soft-spoken, makeup-free, and drab wardrobe of plain jeans and button-down shirt. I see no resemblance to Matt at all.

We stand staring at each other without speaking longer than is socially acceptable, but I haven't decided if I should even let them in yet.

Matt moves me out of their way, and his mom and Wade step into the suite. Seriously, Matt's baby brother has to duck to enter the hotel room. He's not bulked out like Matt, but the height ... shit, I think he might give Shane Miller a run for his money, and that fucker's a giant.

We lead them to the living area, a room with a wide window that overlooks Downtown Nashville.

"Fancy room," his mom says.

Wade hasn't said a word.

"Tell me why you're here," Matt says.

I gesture for them to take a seat on the couch. Matt takes the single armchair. I could pull over one of the stools by the bar area, but I remain standing. More intimidating that way.

My conscience scoffs, because you know, I'm known for my intimidation.

"Your brother wanted to see you," Jennifer says.

Wade looks horrified as if that's a lie or maybe he wasn't prepared for that answer.

"You need more money," Matt counters. He looks to his brother. "You know they're using you as a pawn, right?"

Wade doesn't reply. I don't think he's uttered a word to us the whole day.

"Let me guess, they're already tellin' ya that it's because of you they need to ask me for money."

"He wants to go to Montgomery Academy. That costs money," Jennifer says sweetly.

"I give you enough to cover tuition and expenses."

"Matt, please. He has the brains to go to college, and going to Montgomery Academy will get him into the best."

Which Matt will also pay for, no doubt. I fold my arms across my chest to try to look bigger. Or something. See, totally intimidating.

"Here's the deal ..."

I'm proud of Matt for being composed and appearing like he has the upper hand here, when we both know they hold all the cards. He'll do anything for them.

But he surprises me when he says, "This is the last time I'm gonna bail you and Dad out, and I mean the very last time.

I'm not gonna keep sending you money. I've sent you more than enough over the last seven years, and yet you're in the hole again."

Jennifer balks. "How would you know that?"

"Doesn't matter how I know. Just like I know you and Dad are still going to the track. What I don't know is why you still go with him, unless you have a problem too."

Jennifer breaks down and starts sobbing. I don't know whether to believe the act or not. The cries coming from her mouth sound overdramatic and fake.

"Mom?" Wade asks, his voice surprisingly deep.

"What I'm saying is true," Matt says to his brother. "If I give Mom and Dad the money for your education, I guarantee they'll come up with an excuse as to why you can't go to that school."

"No—" Jennifer starts.

"There are some of the best schools in Chicago."

My breath catches in my throat. When his sister mentioned the possibility of us taking Wade, I knew Matt would think about it. I just didn't think he'd offer it up without talking to me first or thinking it through for more than a few hours.

Although, if I'm honest, a fifteen-year-old seems less daunting than a baby.

And we have discussed it for the last few years on and off.

"No," Jennifer says.

Color me shocked.

"Your father will never go for it."

Wade's head swivels so fast I worry it's going to fall off his skinny, long neck. "That's the first thing you say?"

Oh, wow. Wade and Matt have the same pissed-off tone.

"It's not, *it's up to Wade, you should ask Wade*, maybe

50

Wade has his heart set on Montgomery." He stands. "Your first response should not have been 'You can have him, but we need to negotiate.'"

I feel sorry for the kid, because while he's mad, he doesn't appear all that surprised.

"That ain't what I said," Jennifer yells.

"May as well have been."

I've never seen a giraffe move faster. He storms out, and Jennifer doesn't make a move to go after him.

"Teenagers," I deadpan.

Matt moves to get up and go after his brother, but I step in front of him.

"Don't. You stay and talk with your mom. I'll make sure Wade's okay."

I leave the suite and hit the corridor of the hotel. Only now, I realize I'm going to have to talk to a fucking teenager.

I shake it off.

Pretend he's Jet. A super-tall Jet.

"Yo, wait up." I catch up to him at the elevators just in time to stop him from hitting the call button.

He rolls his eyes. "Is this where you give some prime-time special speech and ask me to run away with you and my brother to play happy gay families?"

Yup. Exactly like Jet. With an added touch of homophobia. Fun.

"You gay too?" I taunt. "That'd be a whole lot easier than trying to sue your parents for custody."

Surprisingly, he's not completely horrified. "I'm confident enough in my heterosexuality that accusing me of being gay isn't gonna rattle me."

"Impressive."

He makes a derisive snort. "It's survival. You think when you and my brother splashed your marriage around the news that we wouldn't deal with the repercussions? I've been defending my sexuality since I was twelve."

"I'm sorry for that," I say and mean it.

Wade eyes me as if trying to figure me out. Good luck, kid. He definitely doesn't come across as a fifteen-year-old and not just the height. He talks like ... like the old white people in my family. I mean, yeah, it's accentuated with his Southern drawl, but where Char and Fern are more stereotypical, Wade seems ... out of place. Like he was born into the wrong family.

"Saw your dad lost the presidential election." He smirks.

And talking politics? Maybe Wade should've been born into *my* family.

"You say that as if I should care. Matt and I had no desire to be swarmed by secret service agents twenty-four hours a day."

"So you decide to adopt genius white-trash kids instead?"

Ooh, living with this guy is gonna be interesting. Jet knows how to dish out attitude as good as he can play guitar, but he's more sarcastic and light. Wade, while being overdramatic, I can hear the resentment in his voice.

Maybe we did make a mistake not doing this sooner—coming here and facing Matt's family once and for all.

"You know your brother would never make you do something you didn't want to, right?" I hope he can hear the sincerity in my voice, because if he's anything like I was at fifteen, no way would I trust anything coming out of a Huntington's mouth. "If you want to stay here and go to your Mont ... whatever Academy, Matt will pay for it. And bail your parents out. Because that's the type of guy Matt is. Offering you a better high school in Chicago and getting you out of Tennessee isn't something we're doing for us, kid. I personally like not having responsibilities."

Wade's eyes dim a little.

"Hey, that's not to say we don't want you to come live with us. Jet did it and now he's as much a brother to me as he is to Matt. But what I mean to say is, this isn't our opportunity to right wrongs or hand out charity—I have my own charity already. This is your opportunity to take hold of a future that Char tells us you really want."

Wade bites his lip. "Mom's right. Dad won't go for it."

"Your parents are addicts, Wade. It may not be an addiction that has visible effects like drugs or alcohol, but they've pissed away hundreds of thousands of dollars in seven years. They're in a bind, and Matt can get them out."

"Using me as a bargaining chip."

"Like I said, that's not for us. It's up to you if you want your tuition paid for maybe a year here—if you're lucky—or a secure future in Chicago with us. Matt would love to have you. Me, I think I'll totally suck at being a parental figure, but hey, I can give it a whirl."

Wade smiles. "You're already better at it than you think."

"Is that a yes, you want to come with us?"

His smile falters. "I still don't see the parentals going for it, but I'm not stupid. I can't pass up the opportunity."

"Then we'll make it happen."

Wade purses his lips. "You know, I always wondered why we struggled for money when Matt's a millionaire and married to a billionaire. Honestly, I thought you guys were assholes."

I laugh. It'll be nice to have that blunt openness back in my life. It seems to run in the Jackson family. "Matt's always been there for you and always will be. If you do decide to stay here, we'll make sure you get the education you deserve, but if you want out, we'll make sure that happens too."

He nods. "Thank you."

The door to our suite opens down the hall, and Jennifer appears. Her cheeks are tear-streaked, her eyes puffy.

"We're going," she grumbles and gives me a dirty look. Maybe Wade is right. There's no way in hell that woman's going to let Wade do what he wants.

I trudge back to the hotel room and find Matt pouring a drink from the minibar. "Didn't go well, I'm guessing?"

"It's gonna cost us."

"How much?"

Matt downs the drink. "Pay off their debts, which is more than I thought possible. I paid off their house with my NFL signing bonus." He pours another drink. "They remortgaged it. They've got nothin'. Less than nothin'."

"It's just money."

"But when does it fucking stop?"

"Probably when Wade turns eighteen and they have no one to hold over your head anymore."

He shakes his head. "I'm gonna make them give up custody. Knowing them, they'll let us take Wade and then call the cops on us or some bullshit."

"Custody could take months."

"He can finish out his sophomore year at his current school, and we'll take him in September. We'll have until then."

Wow, he has it all figured out already.

"So ... it's actually happening."

Matt holds out his drink. "You need this? I didn't really

discuss this with you."

"I'm with you, no matter what." But I take the drink anyway.

"I know a fifteen-year-old isn't a baby, but—"

"It's better," I say. "If I fuck it up, we can blame his childhood."

"Hey, I practically raised that kid for the first few years of his life."

I reach for him and pull him close. "And you did a good job. I only had a ten-minute conversation with him, but he seems like a good guy."

"Are you ready for this?"

"No sweat. It'll be like Jet 2.0."

"This is at least a three-year commitment … you know, in the one city."

Ah, shit. I hadn't thought of that.

Matt chuckles as if the realization is written all over my face. "How do you feel about living in Chicago at least ten months of the year?"

Moving from New York … It won't be a big change— we're already in Chicago half the time—but it's a big step.

I love my city, but I love Matt more.

"Let's do it. We'll move to Chicago permanently."

"I totally expected a bigger fight than this. Or maybe an explosion or freak-out."

I shake my head. "Nope. I'm mature and shit now."

Matt breaks into a full-on laugh this time. "Sure you are."

"Okay, fine. I'm excited to get our cleaning lady back, okay?"

"There's the Noah I know and love."

Damn right.

CHAPTER SEVEN

MATT

L ast week, a phone call from my parents would've made my stomach clench. Not today. If they'd said a week ago they needed to discuss things with me, I would've already had my checkbook out. Not this time.

All these years of wondering if Noah and I did the right thing, the waffling, the convincing ourselves that disrupting my siblings' lives would've been detrimental … all that doubt is gone. Completely.

I got the call this morning that they were willing to negotiate. They said negotiate like Wade's future is something they can barter with, and I didn't hesitate to say yes. Because I'm done. So fucking done.

Last night when Mom told me how deep they've gotten themselves, it was as if the last hold they had on me let go. The cord tying us together severed and the doormat—door-Matt if you will—is no more.

That's how I find myself sitting in my childhood home, a place I haven't stepped foot in for almost a decade. Everything is run-down. The kitchen tiles are coming loose, the carpet's still the same old stained shag, and the whole place smells like cat piss even though they don't have a cat.

It's exactly the way it was when I left.

I don't give them a chance to talk before I'm telling them what the deal is. "You need help. Both of you. I've enabled you for too long, and it's going to stop. I thought I was doing the right thing by supporting you to help my brothers and sisters, but all I've been doing is lining your pockets with more gambling money. And when I cut your allowance by half four years ago, you went and remortgaged a house I'd already paid off. Wade is more responsible than you two, and he's fifteen years old for fuck's sake."

Dad scowls. "You don't get to come in here and—"

"Oh, yes I fucking do. If you want out of this mess, you will listen to what I have to say, and you won't interject or whine about it. Because not only will I drag your asses through the courts, I'll make you pay for you own damn lawyer to fight me."

"What do you want?" Dad says through gritted teeth.

"This is what's going to happen: You're giving up custody of Wade, and he'll come to live with Noah and me in Chicago."

"Wade won't want to live with guys who are … *you*."

"Maybe you've done a shittier job at spreading hate than you'd hoped, or maybe because Wade is so smart he sees through your homophobic bullshit, but we've already spoken to him. He wants to do something great with his life, and Noah and I can provide him with the best education money can buy."

"We won't allow it," Dad says.

"Then I'll sue you for custody, and I will win. Two addicts

who spend all their time and money at the track instead of on their kids? Run-down house versus a spacious penthouse? Two people who care about Wade's future instead of people who only want a way to exploit his future? No contest."

Dad shrugs. "Sue us, then."

I stand. "Good luck paying off the house when your only source of income walks away."

I almost get to the door when Mom finally says something. "Stop."

I pause.

She turns to Dad. "Wade wants to live with them, and we're gonna lose the house. We ain't got a choice."

Dad glances between me and my mother. "Wade!"

My brother appears, because even though they sent him to his room when I arrived, I have no doubt he's been listening this whole time from the hallway.

"You wanna go live with *them*?"

Wade stares at the ground. Growing up with our father, we know his questions are mostly rhetorical.

"You're gonna let them *buy* you?"

That makes Wade's head snap up. "Like *you* can talk. You've taken their money for years."

"I ain't livin' with them," Dad yells. "You're comfortable being under the same roof as a couple of—"

"Finish that sentence," I taunt. "I dare you."

"Yeah, Dad," Wade says. "I'm totally scared of the big gay agenda where they're tryin' to turn everyone to the dark side."

Have I mentioned how much I love my little brother?

One thing I've been worried about was that my parents would mold his brain into thinking the way they do. The fact he's open about it gives me hope that the next generation is smarter than ingrained bigotry.

"Maybe you're just like them," Dad says with venom.

"Then you'll have no problem signing over custody," Wade says easily.

Dad narrows his eyes, not buying it, but surprisingly, he admits defeat. He stands. "Fine. Do what y'all want. I'm goin' out."

He has to pass by me to get to the front door, and as we come face-to-face, just a foot away from each other, our eyes lock.

I smile. "Have fun."

He grumbles something I can't hear as he keeps walking, and as he gets to the door, I decide to throw him one last hard truth.

"Oh, and Dad? This is the last time I pay off your debts. So if you're going to the track, you might wanna think better of it."

His face turns red, his jaw set, and for a brief second, I think he might take a swing at me. But he doesn't. He knows if he does, I'll be gone and the next thing he knows, he'll get a court notice.

It's the first time in my entire life I have held the power when it comes to my parents. Does it suck it's taken twenty-seven years and hundreds of thousands of dollars? Yeah. But this moment? This feeling?

I'm finally free of the burden my parents put on me when I was drafted to the NFL.

CHAPTER EIGHT

NOAH

Matt places a stack of legal papers in front of me at the kitchen table in our New York town house. "These were just couriered over."

"What are they?" It could be anything from something from my charity to an endorsement contract Matt wants an opinion on. It couldn't be the custody papers yet. We were told it's a long process—only made longer if Matt's parents fight it, which if I'm honest, I've been expecting.

But Matt proves me wrong. "It's official. Come September, Wade is ours."

"Wow. That was fast."

"My parents didn't dispute it. My guess is they're desperate for the money."

"Or they want more from you." I don't look my husband in the eyes as I ask, "Are you going to give it to them if they do?"

Matt sighs. "It's tempting, because I still have all that guilt there—that cutting them off would be somehow wrong." He holds his hand up, because he knows I'm about to tell him to stop feeling that way because it's not true. "I know it's not wrong, and I am going to stay strong this time, but it's hard."

I take hold of his hand. "I know it is, baby."

"But, we're finally free of them. I take freedom in the knowledge that I can now tell them to fuck off if I want to, whenever I want to. If I do ever give them money again, it'll be on my terms, not theirs. It's ... liberating."

"So, about that," I hedge. I've been thinking about this for a while, but I didn't want Matt to think I was having doubts about offering Wade a place to stay.

"Oh, God, what are you planning?"

I mock gasp. "I am offended you think it would be something harebrained and irrational."

Matt groans. He loves me, I swear to God. "What is it?"

"We charter a flight with all the guys for our Fiji trip this year and make it a huge group thing."

Hey, look at that. I still have the power to render Matt speechless even after all these years.

"Hear me out. It's going to be the last time we're able to make this trip without a teenager hanging around."

"Exactly. It'll be the last chance to walk around naked and have sex on our private beach. Do you really want the guys there for that?"

"We'll still have our private beach. But we're moving to Chicago. *Chicago*."

"Talon and Miller will be with us in *Chicago*."

"Not during the off-season. They'll be in New York or Denver or doing endorsement shit. And during the season, you guys never want to go out, plus we'll have a kid at home. This is, like, our last chance to live it up for a while. We should make it worth it."

The idea ticks over in his brain, and at least it isn't a flat-out no. "You want … to … and every … wait, *everyone*? Even douchecanoe Bryce?"

"Ugh. I guess he has to come if Soren will. Hey, do you think if we wish hard enough, they'll break up before then?"

"Or we could not invite them."

"Ollie won't like that. He and Soren are tight."

"Yeah, but are we really tight with Soren? He hangs out with us, but it's not like we really know him all that well."

It's true. We hang out all the time, but Soren always seems to be more reserved and hangs out in the background a lot. I don't know what's up with that, but it might have to do with his boyfriend being a pretentious twat.

"We'll invite them," I say. "If I happen to throw Bryce off the flight somewhere over the Pacific, we'll all call it an accident."

Matt leans in and kisses my cheek. "I love it when you get all homicidal."

"Only for you."

He tries to pull away, but I grab the back of his neck and bring his lips back to mine.

After kissing him senseless until neither of us can breathe, I pull back with pure hopefulness in my eyes. "So we're doing it?"

"Fine. Invite everyone. Chances are they can't drop everything eight weeks out anyway and won't come."

My inner evil person is laughing right now, because I'm going to make it happen.

CHAPTER NINE

MATT

"This trip is going to be epic," Noah says from the doorway to our bedroom.

I'm putting the last of my shit in my duffle bag, while Noah's expensive luggage is neatly in a pile by the door.

We still have our poor-guy-rich-guy things that remind us we're so ridiculously different, but instead of seeing that as a bad thing like we did in the beginning, it's amusing to us now.

I've never seen him so excited than he is over this trip to Fiji. He kinda reminds me of Jet with his hyperactive, can't sit still, and talks a million miles a minute charisma he's got going on right now.

It's adorable.

"Wrangling everyone was a feat," I say. "Five athletes, one of the busiest sports agents in New York, and ... well, okay, you, Maddox, and Lennon aren't important people, so it wasn't that hard to organize you guys."

Even my jab can't bring him down.

"Thanks. Just for that, you can fly commercial." Noah's all attitude and gorgeousness.

"You have the worst punishments ever. It's not 'You can't go to Fiji.' It's 'You have to fly first-class ... but commercially.' You're going to make a mean daddy."

Noah winces. "Please don't say *mean daddy* ever again. It does weird things to my brain that I'm not quite sure if I should be disgusted or turned on? Also, you do realize this is our last vacation as childless parents?"

"Soo, as ... people? Is a childless parent like one of those *tree falling in the woods* analogies?"

He playfully shoves me. "You know what I mean."

Yeah, only because he's mentioned it like a billion times.

"I wish Jet could come with us," I say. He was the only one who couldn't come. Well, and Bryce now.

I do not want to be there when karma comes and bites Noah in the ass, because when we'd invited Soren and his boyfriend, and they said yes, my husband decided to start wishing and hoping for their relationship to fall apart. And it did. About two weeks after they agreed to come with us.

There's a good chance Noah might actually control the universe, but I'm so not telling him I think that. His head is big enough as it is.

Noah wraps his arms around me from behind. "With how many times you called him about it, if Jet could make the trip, he would."

"I know."

That doesn't stop me from missing Jet. I know it's horrible for me to think, but I often wish he wasn't killing it. His band has had some number one singles and a decent-selling album, so it's crazy busy for him at the moment.

His tour still has three months to go before he gets to come home, and by then, we'll be back in Chicago for football season ... and forever this time. I'm sure we'll come back to New York when Wade's on summer break, but it won't be the same.

A phone starts vibrating on the bedside table. "That better not be any of the guys canceling or I'm going to be pissed," Noah says.

"Why's it so important for all of them to be there?"

"Last hurrah." Noah's tone drips with *duh*. "Or if I'm speaking jock, think of this as your final play of the game. Everyone should be there for it."

I never thought I'd see the day where Noah—snobby, cares about no one else but himself Noah—would be choosing to spend his last vacation as a childless parent, as he puts it, with a group of guys. They're the best guys in the world, there's no doubt about that, but even though Noah has always been surrounded by people, he's always been a bit of a lone wolf.

Maybe he's realizing he's thirty now and finally needs to grow up and needs one last drunken two-week party. If that's the case, I'll give it to him. He's given me everything, and he's about to give up New York for me. I'll give him whatever ridiculous thing he asks for.

"It's not like we'll never have a vacation alone," I say. "Wade is fifteen. He'll be at college in three years."

"That's twenty-one in gay years," Noah singsongs.

"You're confusing that with dog years."

He can't hear me as he answers his phone.

I assume the call has something to do with Rainbow Beds, but when his voice cracks, my gaze flies to his.

"What's wrong?" I mouth.

He says a few mm-hmms and uh-huhs, sounding in deep concentration. When the phone call ends, he gives an extremely polite "Thank you very much" and that's when I know it's big.

Noah. Polite. To anyone who isn't me.

Yep. It's a world-ending event.

My husband stares at his phone long after the screen goes black.

"What is it?"

"Holy shit." Noah stumbles back and sits on the edge of our bed. "Holy shit!"

I rush to his side. "What? You're freaking me out."

"You know how the adoption agency said it shouldn't take as long to find a match for us, but then nothing happened so we figured we'd be waiting the few years like everyone else, so when the Wade thing happened, we didn't take our names off the list?"

My heart skips a beat completely before it drops into my stomach. "Yeah …"

"There's … there's a birth mom who's about six months along. She wants to meet us."

It's my turn to stumble toward the bed for support. "A … a baby."

"And a teenager," Noah says, his eyes wide. "Like, at the same time."

The quick panic of *we're not ready* hits for a microsecond before a seed of excitement grows in my gut.

Yeah, plans changed when we offered to take in Wade, but the baby thing has still been on the agenda. We just thought it'd be a future thing.

But one look at Noah, and I know this might not happen. His expression is a mix of panic and nauseated.

"We both still want this, right?" I ask.

I'm expecting a no.

Instead, Noah breaks out into the biggest grin I've ever seen on him. Seriously, it takes up most of his face.

"Fuck yes," Noah says.

My brows shoot up to my hairline. "Yes? Like, yes, yes?"

"Yes, yes. Again, fuck yes. I mean, I'm freaking out, don't get me wrong, but I haven't thought of anything else since we decided to do this."

I let out a breath of relief. "Me too."

His face falls the tiniest bit. "Wait, will Wade be okay with this?"

He'll have to be is my immediate response, but we should be sure. "Let's call him."

One thing I have loved since standing up to my parents is access to my siblings. I keep in contact with all of them except for Daisy, who's firmly on the conservative side of the family. Maybe her rich fiancé can take over paying for Mom and Dad's habits.

I wish I could say Daisy's disapproval doesn't get to me, but it does. I just keep repeating in my head what Noah says: four out of five ain't bad, and I guess with our upbringing, he's right. It's probably amazing that only one followed our parents' views.

We Skype Wade, our faces close together so he can see us both when he answers, and he picks up with smirk on his face.

"Aren't you guys on your way to Fiji?"

"Soon," I say. "But we just got a pretty important phone call we want to talk to you about."

He frowns. "Okay?"

"How would you feel sharing an apartment with a baby?" Noah asks.

"I've already prepared myself to live with Matt."

"Funny," I grumble. "But seriously. We, uh, looked into adoption a few months before we asked you to move in with us, but we thought it would take years."

His frown is back. "Oh." He stares off camera, and I can see his Adam's apple bounce.

"What's wrong?" I ask.

"Like, you're getting a baby now, so you won't want me hanging—"

"Stop." My stern tone takes him off guard. "Wade, we're calling to ask if you're okay with moving in with a baby. We're not trying to back out of taking you in. At all. We promised you, and you're a part of this family now. Not the family we grew up in." I wrap my arm around Noah. "This family. You have a say."

"And if I say no?" His voice is quiet. "That a baby will interfere with my studies because they cry lots and grow into toddlers who destroy shit, and they're loud—"

"Maybe we should rethink this baby thing," Noah says, but he's laughing as he says it.

I nudge him and turn to my brother. "Wade, if you say no, we'll tell the adoption agency that we're not ready, and we'll reapply in a few years after you're in college."

A shy smile twists at Wade's lips. "Okay."

"Okay?" I ask.

"I'm cool with the baby thing," he clarifies. "It's your life, you're giving me more opportunities than staying in Tennessee will, and I'm not going to take that for granted."

I narrow my eyes. "But you felt the need to test our loyalty by saying no first?"

He brings his hand up and pinches his thumb and fore-finger together. "A little?"

"Fair enough." I turn to Noah. "So, we're really doing this."

His blue-green eyes glimmer. "We're doing this."

"And you have a plane to catch," Wade says.

Noah squeezes my hand. "Yeah, we do."

We hang up with Wade, a weight lifted off my shoulders, but Noah still looks panicked.

"What's wrong?"

Noah stares up at me. "This really is going to be our final play now."

I shake my head. "Nah. This is just the beginning of our second half." My big romantic label is scoffed at.

"Jock talk." Noah stands in a flurry, that overexcited puppy thing happening again. "Whatever we're calling it, it's going to be totally *epic*."

Yeah. Epic.

The beginning of the rest of our lives.

II

MADDOX AND DAMON

CHAPTER TEN

DAMON

I stare out at the tarmac from the private charter lounge at LAX, my phone to my ear. I'm already freaking out. Not about this vacation, which is long overdue, but what's going to happen at work while I'm gone. "I'll have my phone on the whole time. Call me if you have any questions, any concerns, any—"

"Boss," my assistant says, her voice still bubbly even though I'm being neurotic as hell and she has to be over it already.

We haven't even left the States yet. It's been one flight. New York to L.A.

I almost don't want to get on the next leg of the trip, but I have to. It's the first break I'm getting from the firm since I was given my full-time job. That was four years ago.

"I can handle it," Carly says.

I know she can. She's a competent undergrad, studying her way up like I did. It's why I hired her. She reminded me of … well, me. That, and nine out of every ten employees in this field are men. Straight men. Carly was as qualified and eager as the others I interviewed, so I wanted to give her a chance that others in this industry might not.

This vacation came at the perfect moment where classes are out for the summer, so she can take on this responsibility. And there are plenty of other seasoned agents there to help her out if she gets stuck.

"It's going to be okay," I say.

"I know," Carly says.

"I wasn't talking to you."

"Talking to yourself is the first sign of insanity."

I huff a laugh. "Oh, I was already there years ago. Call me if you need anything. Like, *anything*. I'm expecting a deal for Soren to come through, and he'll be with me, so—"

"Stop stressing. It's all good. I'll keep you in the loop. Now, go get some sun."

"I will. Right after this gazillion-hour-long trip."

Why do Matt and Noah do this to themselves every year? Why not Hawaii? Bermuda? Somewhere so much friggin' closer.

"Have fun with that," she sings and ends the call.

Everything will be fine, I tell myself again. Unless one of my players gets arrested or pushed out of any closets, Carly can handle it. And let's face it, my most "problematic" clients are coming on this "*final play*" with me.

I have to laugh at Noah for inviting us all on this trip. Now that he and Matt are taking in Matt's youngest brother, he seems to think his social life is somehow over for the next few years.

Then again, the thought of running around after a fifteen-year-old during a rebellious phase does sound exhausting.

Though, the impression I get of Wade is he's got a good head on his shoulders. According to Matt, anyway. We haven't met the kid yet.

Maddox's arms wrap around me from behind, and his lips land on the back of my neck. "Everything okay?"

"Perfect."

"Please don't tell me one of your players got a DUI or something and you're going back to New York."

I spin in his arms. "Nothing like that. Just me being anal about everything."

Maddox snorts. "Which is funny, because you don't do that."

With any other guy, I'd assume that's a jab at my lack of versatility, but I know it's not with Maddox. He literally finds it amusing.

It's still funny to me that it's the "straight" guy who understands my lack of desire to bottom most. I have offered, but he has always said he won't make me do anything in the bedroom that doesn't get me off, and the same goes for him. If he doesn't like something, I don't make him do it.

And anytime I say I feel guilty for not reciprocating, Maddox takes off all his clothes and rides my dick until my vision blurs and he falls apart for me. Sometimes I say it just because I know it'll lead to sex.

I have the best guy in the whole fucking world, and if reminding me that Carly can handle everything isn't enough to get me on that plane, knowing I'm giving something to Maddox he's always wanted is.

When we got together, I promised him we'd travel the world.

Where I go, he goes. But when I'm stuck working seventy-hour weeks with no vacation time, the farthest we go is to his hometown in Pennsylvania to visit family or to Boston to see his sister.

This trip, though, is about us and going back to where it all started—making a promise to each other to see as much of the world as we can, be with each other, and have fun.

Naked fun, island fun, drunken fun, we're excited for it all.

Maddox licks his lips, and his blue eyes shine up at me. "You know what I was thinking?"

"Uh-oh, here's trouble."

"Not trouble. I was thinking we could knock something off the bucket list today."

"Yeah?"

His lips land near my ear. "I've always wanted to join the mile-high club."

I groan, and my cock thickens in my jeans. "Where's a plane? Like right now …"

Maddox puts his head on my shoulder. "Soon. I think they said we'll be boarding in twenty minutes."

"Twenty minutes? I can't wait that long." I grab his hand and start dragging him toward the restrooms, but he stops me.

"Uh-uh. It only counts if the plane is in the air. Airport sex is not romantic or mile-high-ish."

"I hate you," I grumble. "You can't mention sex and then tell me I have to wait."

"Twenty minutes," Maddox repeats in a stern voice.

I love that stern voice. He barely ever has to use it because he's so carefree and laid-back, but when he does …

I pull him against me so he can feel how hard I am. When he gazes up at me, I cock my eyebrow in challenge.

"It's not just twenty minutes," I say. "We won't be able to

get out of our seat for takeoff. Then we won't exactly be able to rush for the bathroom immediately ..."

I think I'm winning, but I'm really not.

Maddox smiles and pats my cheek. "The more we wait, the more explosive it will be on the plane."

Since when the fuck is my boyfriend into edging?

He pulls away from me, and we head back to the group.

Reluctantly.

Lennon and Ollie are looking at a travel book on Fiji, Talon and Miller are by the windows watching the planes come in and take off over the other side of the airport, Matt and Noah are Skyping one of Matt's sisters, and Soren's lying across one of the couches, his arm over his eyes, and with headphones on.

Poor Soren.

He's coming on this trip with all couples after being recently dumped by his long-term boyfriend. I'm in the middle of trying to negotiate a new contract for him in the NHL, and he's nearing retirement age. He's after a no-trade clause, but because of his age, his team is reluctant. His life is a bit of a mess right now, but hopefully this vacation will pull him out of his funk.

We sit in the lounge waiting for our plane to be ready ... well, Maddox sits. I kind of squirm around in my seat.

Maddox scoffs. "Someone's so impatient."

"Someone's a tease."

He leans over and kisses along my jaw. "It's not really teasing when you know I'll follow through, is it?"

I shift again, lifting my hips off the couch to try to get comfortable with this damn hard-on that I'm trying to hide in my jeans. "It is when you drag it out."

Maddox keeps kissing his way across my skin. "Just think how hot it's gonna be. You pushing inside me while I grip onto whatever I can." His hand moves up my thigh, and my gaze darts around the small lounge to make sure none of the guys are watching. They're all too involved in their own shit. "You having to cover my mouth to stop me from screaming out. And then no matter how hard we clean up afterward, you know I'm still gonna be covered in our cum all the way to F—"

I cut him off with my mouth on his and my hand cupping the back of his neck.

He groans, and that must be what gets the others' attention because Noah's voice cuts across the room.

"Nope. No way."

Maddox pulls away and glares at Noah. "No way, what?"

Noah stands. "Actually, this goes for all of you. You're under strict instructions to keep it in your pants on the rented plane. No mile-high shenanigans. There are cameras and shit on board. And I'm sure the last thing Damon needs on this vacation is any TMZ news of a sex tape featuring any of his clients."

I wonder if anyone will care if it's my sex tape ... I shake my head. Damn it, I need to be professional.

"What if it's a solo sex tape?" Soren quips.

"Don't even," I say. "I need to not work for the next two weeks. Please."

There are rounds of complaints, even from Matt, so I'm guessing we were all planning to get a little action thirty thousand feet in the air.

Noah's tiny Gulfstream jet isn't big enough to get us to Fiji, so we chartered a flight ... well, Noah and Matt did, because they have hundreds of thousands of dollars at their fingertips. We're just along for the ride.

I'm disappointed Maddox won't get his mile-high wish, but that means we can take care of my predicament right now.

I stand and pull Maddox up with me. "We'll be right back."

Maddox laughs.

And, of course, that's when our fucking flight crew comes through the doors to greet us and take us to the plane.

Eleven motherfucking hours.

Kill me now.

The low hum of the engine filters through the cabin of the plane. The lights are off, shades drawn, and we're each sprawled out on our own reclining seat.

Soren scored a couch-style seat in front of us because each of us couples argued over which one of us would take it.

Everyone else is sleeping, and someone's even snoring. Don't know who though.

I'm frustrated, uncomfortable, and it's been about five hours so far of me trying to convince my cock to stay down.

Maddox's hand lands on my thigh underneath a blanket we're sharing. Our seats are close enough to each other to reach, but there're armrests in the way for anything more to happen, no matter how desperate I am.

I turn my head toward him and see his bright blue eyes shining at me in the dim light.

"I can feel your frustration from all the way over here, and I can't sleep because of it," he whispers.

"Sorry."

He leans across the small gap between our seats. "Don't be sorry. Let's do something about it."

I glance around the small cabin, remembering the cameras and making sure all the guys are asleep. "You wanna join the mile-high club that much?"

"No. We're not having sex, but I thought I could help you out." Maddox's hand moves up my thigh and cups my cock over my pants.

I immediately harden to the point of pain, as if my dick is screaming, "Yes, finally!"

My hands scramble under the blanket and undo my seat belt and the button on my jeans, while Maddox goes for my fly.

With my cock free, Maddox wraps his fingers around me, only making me harder and needier. I lift a knee and rest my foot on the edge of my seat so the blanket rises off our laps and hides what he's doing underneath it.

He's leaning over, so his cheek is right by my mouth. I kiss my way along his jaw and down his neck and love it when his breath hitches.

My lips move up toward his ear. "I love you, Maddy," I say, speaking low.

"You're only saying that because my hand is on your dick, but I love you too."

Maddox's thumb swipes over my slit and moves down my shaft.

My chest heaves, and I try to catch my breath.

With how hard up I've been, I know I'm not going to last long.

"Kiss me," I beg.

Maddox's mouth meets mine, his tongue lapping at my lips

to let him in. When I do, I have to bite back a moan, because this needs to be quiet.

I get lost in my boyfriend, his mouth, and the way his hand works me over. I'm teetering on the edge between letting go and that awesome sensation of an orgasm you know is coming but not quite there yet.

My thoughts get fuzzy, and the sound of the jet engines amplifies until it's all I can hear.

So when Maddox's hand stills, I'm confused.

"Wha?" I say, still half in my blissed-out haze.

"As much as I'm enjoying the free porn show, I kind of don't want to know what my agent sounds like when he blows his load."

I freeze at Soren's words. "Go back to sleep, then."

"Never was asleep, jackass. Can you guys seriously not wait eleven measly hours to get it on?"

"For your information, it's been over a week," Maddox hisses. "Damon's been working overtime to make sure he could even come on this trip."

"Aww, a whole week? Try months and then complain to me."

"What's going on?" Noah croaks from the other side of the plane.

"Nothing," I say, a little too quickly. Just have my cock out. Nothing to see here.

Maddox starts laughing beside me and goes back to his side, taking his hand with him.

I was so close. So fucking close.

Now my dick is softening, disappointed again.

"I swear as soon as we get to the island, your ass is mine," I growl.

"Again, still not asleep," Soren says.

I tuck myself away under the blanket and throw my head back.

I already hate Fiji.

———————

I fucking love Fiji.

It's not the bright orange sunset that's happening right outside our hut. It's not the smell of salt water and ocean or the nice cool breeze.

It's my boyfriend flat on his stomach, naked, with me pushing his head into a pillow while I thrust into him over and over and over again.

Between the long-ass flight and being cockblocked at every chance, Maddox was right: it has made this more explosive.

Only problem with that is I don't know how much longer I'm going to last, and Maddox is taking everything I'm giving him with no indication he's anywhere near close to the finish line.

"Are you close?" I rasp. "You're so tight. So hot. Fuck, I love you. You need to come. Like right now. Or soon. Like, hurry up."

Maddox laughs. "You really are close. You ramble when you're—" I peg his prostate "—fuck! Right there."

I do it again and again until Maddox mutters unintelligible things.

"I'm gonna come," I warn.

"Take me with you."

There's no room between him and the bed to reach for his

cock, so all I can do is thrust harder and hope the friction beneath him is enough to push him over the edge.

Only problem with that is it brings me that much closer and I might beat him to the punch.

Baseball stats run through my head, trying to stave off my impending orgasm.

Sweat drips from my hair and down my torso, making our skin clammy and slick. My hand in Maddox's blond hair is wet, and a bead of perspiration falls down the side of his face.

He finally puts me out of my misery by making that face of his—the one where his eyes roll back, his mouth drops open, and he lets out a sound that makes my balls draw up tight and my cock pulse.

I spill inside him, collapsing on top of him as I do.

Maddox recovers first and grunts, his telltale sign he needs me to get up.

"Can't ... move ..." I pant.

"Have to. We'll be late for dinner."

"Fuck dinner."

"Can't go another round yet," he jokes.

I pull out of him, flopping onto my back. "Who cares if we're late. We're on vacation. We can do what we want."

"We should at least make an appearance on the first night. Matt and Noah are footing the bill for all of us to hang out here."

"Fine," I grumble. "But if we told them what we were doing, they'd totally understand."

"And imagine if we all did that? Poor Soren's gonna be sitting in the dining hut all by himself."

"Yeah, well, after that flight, he can totally fend for himself."

Maddox gets out of bed and pulls me up. "Come on. Quick shower, dinner and drinks, and then maybe I'll let you blow me when we get back."

"How generous of you," I say dryly but don't mean it. At all. I'll be rushing through dinner just to get my mouth wrapped around Maddox's cock.

He leads me to the bathroom, but the second we cross the threshold, I get a shiver running up my spine and the keen sense of eyes on me. Eyes that don't belong to Maddox.

When I turn, on the glass of the shower door is a giant-ass spider.

I'll admit my next move errs on the side of cowardice.

Something that can only be described as a scream that would send dogs crazy within a five-mile radius leaves my mouth, and I run for shelter. Why my brain thinks standing on top of the toilet can save me, I have no idea, but the next thing I know, I'm there.

Meanwhile, Maddox is laughing so hard, he has to hold on to his stomach.

I can't do anything but point at the eight-legged spawn of Satan.

The spider crawls toward me, and I scream again.

"Shh," Maddox says though still laughing. "The whole island will hear you, and then we'll have everyone busting through the damn door, and we're both naked and covered in cum."

"Get it." Why is he not killing the spider that's right next to him? More importantly, why isn't he freaking out? We're in *Fiji*.

Maybe it wants to kill us.

With a swift move, Maddox finds his flip-flop by the door

and flattens that fucker. "Want to come give your hero a kiss for saving your life?"

"Fuck you."

"Nah, we just did that. Dinner and drinks, remember?"

I grumble throughout the shower and the whole way to dinner.

"You're late," Soren taunts as we enter the food hut.

In his defense, we are the last ones here.

"Shut it, Canada," Maddox says.

Poor Soren—a Canadian living in New Jersey. He's the butt of most of Maddox's jokes when they're in the same room.

Secretly, I think Soren loves it though. He always shrugs it off, because he knows Maddox is only joking even if he claims not to be.

"This is Damon's first proper vacation in four years. We're making the most of it," Maddox says.

"I would too," Soren mumbles and takes a sip from his liquor-filled coconut.

"We need to get Soren laid," Noah announces. "Where can we find some Fijian rent boys?"

Soren chokes on his drink and splutters everywhere.

"Not a good idea," Joni, the owner of this island, says. "Very illegal in Fiji. Unless you like jail."

"Soren might like jail considering his dry spell," Ollie says.

"Don't … need … a prostitute," Soren says in between coughing. "Thanks though."

Matt turns to Talon and Miller. "You guys used to have threesomes all the time. Maybe you can throw Soren a bone."

"Totally would," Miller says, "but it turns out Talon's one possessive motherfucker. Sorry."

Talon winks at Soren.

When everyone at the table laughs, I feel kinda bad for him.

He asks for another drink.

"You do need to get over what's-his-face," I say to him.

He holds up his coconut. "That's what this is for."

"Come wakeboarding with us tomorrow," Miller says. "That'll take your mind off him."

"I was thinking of going for a hike to the top of the headland."

Beside me, Maddox tenses.

"Hey, aren't you guys doing that?" Matt asks us.

We are? That's news to me.

"No," Maddox says quickly. "I mean … we are, but … like …"

"They're gonna have sex up there," Noah says, and Maddox tenses more.

I have no idea what's going on with him right now, and I don't get the chance to ask him to give me an explanation.

Ollie leans in closer to Soren. "For what it's worth, Bryce wasn't the right guy for you."

"I know," Soren says, but he doesn't look convinced.

"He didn't even like hockey," Ollie adds.

"I don't like hockey," Lennon points out, "but I'm not a dick about it like him."

"You love hockey," Ollie says. "You're just stubborn about admitting it."

"Guys," Maddox says, "we're not getting into the sports debate again."

Despite Maddox saying not to start a debate, of course, we do.

"None of you guys have the stamina to go nine plus innings," I say.

"Any sport where you only need to wear a cup as padding can't be classed a superior sport," Talon argues, and the other two football players agree.

I'm not having that. "Says the people who only have to play a maximum twenty-two weeks of the year."

Ollie and Soren look at each other as if having a silent conversation.

Then Ollie nods and turns to us all. "All I have to say is, if we were to put ice skates on you assholes, you'd all fall on your faces. We could hold our own playing your sports. Also, twenty-six weeks in the regular season, bitches. Then another nine for the Cup. Bow down to your wicked cool superiors." He nudges Soren.

"Yeah, what he said."

"I can't believe we're having this discussion again," Noah says.

"I told them not to start it," Maddox agrees.

I wrap my arm around Maddox. "As the only two non-sporting people here, you guys get no opinion."

"Yeah, yeah, yeah," Maddox says. "You're all big, bad athletes. Do any of you other badasses scream high-pitched at a spider in the bathroom?"

"We're in *Fiji*," I emphasize. "What if Fiji's like Australia and all the wildlife is trying to kill you?"

Everyone laughs at me, of course, and I'm happy I'm the focus of mockery instead of Soren.

Even so, he says he needs some air and excuses himself. He's a little wobbly on his feet. Maybe he drank too much too fast.

I go to stand to go after him, but Ollie beats me to it.

"I'll go."

More mockery occurs in their absence, mainly at me and the masculine way in which I handle spiders.

The food is great, the drinks even better, and it's not long until I forget I'd rather be locked away in a hut with Maddox.

But our banter is cut off by the rhythmic sound of a chopper flying above us.

"Paparazzi?" Maddox asks.

"We're in Fiji," Noah says. "Paparazzi don't care about us here."

The sound overhead gets louder, as if coming in for landing.

"And what paparazzi have helicopters?" I ask.

There's a brief moment where we all stare at each other before we jump out of our seats and rush to the edge of the hut.

Soren and Ollie come from the direction of the beach, also wondering what's going on.

Stepping off the helicopter is none other than Jet Jackson himself—Matt's younger brother and rising rock star. He's Jet to us, but to the world he's Jay from Radioactive.

Considering he wasn't supposed to be here, after greetings and hugs are given out, he joins us and sits at the end of the table and shovels food in his mouth like it's completely normal for him to be in a foreign country for no reason.

"We're waiting," Matt says.

Jet lifts his head. "Huh?" His mouth is full of half-chewed food.

"Your tour?" Noah asks. "Concert dates, no time off, no rest for the famous. All your words."

"Fiji must not get the news. Rest of Radioactive's part of the tour's been canceled."

"Why?" Matt asks.

Jet chews and swallows hard. "Well, it's gonna be all over social media soon enough, so you may as well know now. I have nodes. Need to rest my voice."

Everyone glances around the table at each other, because I don't think any of us are buying what the kid's selling.

We all love Jet like a little brother, but this vacation is only two weeks. I want to make the most of it without getting involved in rock star drama.

I'll leave that for Matt to handle.

CHAPTER ELEVEN

MADDOX

My palms are all itchy from being covered in sweat, and it's not the humid Fijian air causing it. Or the exertion from climbing this stupid mountain. I'd blame Damon for being all sport-like and outdoorsy, but this was my idea. Damon's plan for this vacation basically consisted of one thing: lots and lots of naked time in bed.

Normally, I'd be all over that, but not here. Not with what I have planned.

I'm excited about reaching the top of the headland, not so excited about what I'm going to do once we get up there.

Four years, I've been with Damon now. I've been in a committed adult relationship for four years. Give me a fucking medal. Please.

Considering I used to run away at the first sign of even being labeled as someone's boyfriend, being here with a ring burning a hole in my pocket is almost unbelievable. I wouldn't believe it myself if I wasn't me.

My heart may be pounding, my breathing not coming out quite right, but I'm ready for this. I'm totally ready for—

I trip on a tree root.

Motherfucker!

My hand flies out to try to stop me from face-planting, but instead of reaching its intended target—Damon—my hand flails and lands on some weird-ass spiky plant.

I let out a very manly high-pitched scream as I fall to the ground. My right shoulder and side slam into the rough forest floor.

My hand is stinging like all fuck.

"Shit, are you okay?" Damon's at my side in an instant, pulling me up, but that doesn't comfort me any.

"I'd believe your concern more if you weren't trying not to laugh," I grumble.

Damon clears his throat and smothers his smile. "Sorry."

"No, you're not! You're still trying not to laugh."

His grin is still sexy, even if he's thirty now. He does not appreciate the old-man comments though. Shocking, really.

"I really am sorry." Damon cups my face.

He leans in and kisses me, the familiar taste and jolt of feels shooting down my spine still ever present. Every time he kisses me, I remember what it was like to kiss him that very first time on a random dance floor at a random wedding in my hometown.

It's like standing on the edge of a cliff, waiting to free fall off the side. It's like chasing something I think is unattainable only to be reminded I already have it.

It's happiness.

When he breaks the kiss, putting distance between us

again, I want to pull him closer, but when I reach for him, my swelling hand catches my attention.

Damon hisses and grabs my wrist. "What did you fall on?"

"It's nothing. I'm fine. We're close to the top, so let's keep going."

"Babe, I don't think that's nothing. You're bleeding."

Ah, that must be the tiny little red dots all over my hand.

"What did you touch?"

"I don't know. Some spiky plant." I point beside me.

Damon goes to check it out while I wiggle my fingers and see the spots on my hand dance.

"Are there, like, poisonous things in Fiji?"

"Fuck," Damon says again and comes back to my side. "We need to get you back to the main house."

"No!" Fucking stupid, prickly plant, proposal-blocking me. I shake out my hand which stings like a motherfucker. "It's fine." I wince. "See?"

I had a plan, damn it. A good one.

We were gonna climb to the lookout at the top of the mountain on this private island. When Matt and Noah asked our entire group of friends to come on their yearly vacation this time, we didn't question it. I was too busy researching a way to ask Damon to be mine forever. The perfect way, because he deserves it.

God knows these past four years haven't been perfect, but I wouldn't change them for anything.

Damon's been busy building his client list, while I've been saving up money to go on vacations around the world. This is the first trip we've been able to have since we went to Bermuda a few years back.

Not that I'm complaining about that as hard as I thought I

would, because even though I want to see other countries, my entire world is the man beside me. There's nothing stopping me from traveling on my own, but if I've learned anything over the last four years, it's been that Damon makes everything better.

And if I have it my way, we'll have the rest of our lives together to do what we want. Travel, buy more property, be awesome uncles to our sisters' kids.

I always used to think being tied down to someone would stifle my opportunity at a carefree life. Responsibilities, kids, marriage … it all felt like a heavy weight—the old ball and chain.

A life with Damon? Responsibilities aren't daunting, and we've both agreed we don't want kids. Marriage … well, I'm compromising, because he's worth it.

"We're going back," he says as he stalks away toward the ugly-ass plant that assaulted me and takes a photo. "Do you need help? Can you walk?"

"I hurt my hand, not my foot."

With a nod, he heads the opposite way on the trail, going down the mountain.

"I'm fine," I call out to him. "We should keep going." I can't let a sore hand ruin this.

"Sure, and when you die from all the poison running through your system, I'll throw you off the cliff. Quick burial."

"Well, that's morbid," I mumble and reluctantly follow him. "Love you too."

It only takes Damon glancing back at me once for me to decipher the look of determination on his face is actually panic.

I reach for him with my good hand. "Damon."

He pushes forward.

"Baby!" My tone is supposed to be authoritative, but it doesn't quite have the effect I want.

Damon spins on his heel. "Shit, are you in pain? Are you faint? Do you need me to go ahead and get someone to come back with a first aid kit, or I dunno … anti-venom or something?"

I can't help laughing as I step closer and press myself against him. "I'm fine. My hand's a little tingly, but that's all."

"What if the tingly feeling is poison or you're having an allergic reaction or—"

I grunt. "Fiji might not even have poisonous plants."

"Do you know how close we are to Australia? Everything tries to kill you on this side of the world."

I roll my eyes. "Australia is another four-hour flight away with plenty of ocean between us. I know because I looked at possibly extending our vacation to go there, but you needed to get back to work."

Okay, that might've come out more bitter than I intended.

Damon frowns. "Are you really bringing that up now while you're dying from a poison plant?"

"I'm not dying."

"You don't know that."

"You're impossible when you're worrying." I try to reach for my phone in my pocket, but it's in my right one, and my right hand is sore as fuck, and trying to get to it with my left is impossible.

Damon huffs. "What are you doing?"

"Trying to reach my phone to google it so you're not stressing at me for the hike back."

Damon's hand goes straight into my pocket, and I realize

my critical mistake a moment too late. I put my phone in my left, so I could reach for the ring with my right. The bulge in my shorts isn't my phone but the fucking ring.

"Wait!" I yell and try to step back, but it's already done.

Damon's eyes widen as he wraps his fingers around the small box. "Maddy ... what ... what is ..." He pulls it out of my pocket completely. "Is this ..."

"Motherfucking twatwaffle on a stick, I messed this up."

"Babe?"

I sigh. "The plan was to walk up this stupid mountain, and while looking out at the stupid ocean with a stupidly majestic view, I'd get down on one knee and ask you to be mine forever. It was going to be beautiful, damn it!"

Damon looks between me and the ring box and back again. "Is this real?"

I slowly step forward and pull him against me with my good hand. "You're the kind of guy who likes to have things in order. You want boxes ticked, every i to be dotted, and every t to be crossed. I know you want marriage, and I want to give you everything." I lower my voice. "Marry me."

Damon's mouth works open and closed like a fish. "Poison."

My eyebrows shoot up in surprise. "Not really the answer I was expecting."

Damon holds up his finger. "We just ... I dunno ... just pause."

"You can't pause a proposal."

"Well, I just did." Damon gets out his own phone and taps at the screen. Then scrolls. Then taps away again. "Okay. Sooo, I may have overreacted. No poisonous plants in Fiji."

"I think the fact I'm not dead yet would already tell you that. Or at least that the one I fell on isn't poisonous."

Damon shakes it off and stares at me, pinning me with those green eyes I fell in love with so many years ago. "Okay, so the proposal thing—"

"Marry me," I say again. This time I lift the lid of the box and show off the simple titanium band Stacy helped me pick out.

"Oh, babe." Damon's eyes soften.

The expectation of a yes rings in my head, but that is not what I hear.

"No."

My face falls. "What?"

"We're not getting married." Damon looks so serious, and it cuts through my heart like a knife.

Is he unhappy? Does he think he's holding me back by working so much? Does he—

"I love you, Maddy. For so many reasons we'd be here until sundown if I listed them all. You're my forever, my everything, my future, and I don't need a piece of paper to tell me that. You're right when you say I like things in order. I like boxes and hard lines. But you? You make my life messy in the best possible way. You remind me that there's more to life than rules and labels and everything being perfect."

I purse my lips. "Totally sounds like you just said I'm messy and not perfect, but that can't be right."

Damon laughs. "That right there is why I love you more than words can say. Why I want to spend the rest of my life with you. Just, not as your husband. Refusing to get married is almost like … I don't know how to explain it. It's like giving that uptight side of me the finger. Not to mention you don't want to do this. Not really. You're doing it for me, not for *us*. You're more anti-marriage than you are anti-New Jersey. And that's saying something."

"I'm so glad after all these years you finally acknowledge my Jersey hate for what it is."

"Oh, it's still ridiculous, but I know there's no changing your mind."

"True love." I glance away and swallow hard. "But I do actually want this. I mean, maybe not the wedding, because the thought of having to organize that shit makes me break out in hives, but the marriage. You and me. I want us. Forever."

Damon's lips meet mine in a slow, burning kiss. "You've always been mine, and nothing's going to change that." He takes the ring and slips it on his finger. "Oooh, look at that. We just got married on the side of a mountain in Fiji."

"That doesn't count."

Damon shrugs. "Just giving myself the finger again. I don't need the wedding to know it's going to be me and you until the day we die."

I bite my lip. Relief isn't what I'm supposed to be feeling right now, is it? I mean, I totally get what Damon is saying, because it's exactly how I feel. And he's right. I am doing this more for him than me or us. If he'd said yes, of course I'd go through with it, because I love him.

"You're thinking way too hard about this," Damon says. "I can practically hear your thoughts running through that head of yours."

"Sorry. I just … I was kinda expecting you to say yes. My ego is bruised, but my heart is full, so I have no idea what to do right now."

"Kiss me? That's a good thing to do right now."

He still loves my mouth, and as I kiss him again, it feels like more—like a promise of nothing yet forever at the same time.

I pull back. "No wedding?"

"No wedding."

"Okay, but you're the one who's gonna have to tell my parents and Stacy, because they'll never believe it was you who chickened out."

Damon grins. "I'm okay with that." He stares down at my bloodied hand. "We really should go get that checked out. You may not be dying, but it doesn't look good."

"What, no celebratory *We're not getting married* blowjobs?"

"Later. Promise."

CHAPTER TWELVE

DAMON

Maddox's hand is fine, and the second Joni and Ema, the owners of the place we're staying at on the island, tell us that, I have Maddox naked and riding my cock.

His hot, tight ass always makes me lose a few brain cells, but being balls-deep in him while he straddles my lap and stares at me with a spark or feeling we've never shared before, I can't help thinking his proposal has changed everything, even though it has changed nothing.

We're still not getting married, and even though I'll proudly wear his ring, we're not engaged. Yet, I can't help seeing him in a different light. A new light. After four years together, I didn't think that was possible.

Maybe I've been subconsciously waiting for Maddox to freak out again like he did when we first got together. I was definitely worried around the time we bought our place in Brooklyn. Sharing real estate is a big fucking deal, and even though it was my commission from signing Matt and Ollie that paid for the place, I waited for Maddox to put up a fight when I said I wanted it to be ours and I was putting his name on the deed too. But the only concern he expressed was about the mold growing in the spare bedroom. And even then, all he said about it was "That can be your office. I'm too good-looking to die young."

Maddox giving me this—a promise of forever with a symbol instead of just words—makes the way he's looking at me so much more intense.

Every time I thrust upward into his body and he grinds down on my cock, I can feel the forever being promised.

Maddox is mine, and he always will be.

I've been lucky with my career, and I know I owe most of that to Maddox because of his connections to Matt and Ollie. Because of Ollie, I've signed Caleb Sorensen, and because of Matt, I've also signed Shane Miller and the biggest quarterback in the NFL, Marcus Talon.

It's why I've been feeling guilty toward Maddox lately. I'm always working, and it always seems like I'm promising him a future where we get to share in his dream of traveling the world, only to say, "Sorry, babe, I have to fly across the country to scout another client." There has to be a happy medium, but I haven't found it yet.

With my five big clients and a couple of up-and-comers, I don't really have to worry much about my job, but it's finding the time in between all my clients' drama to actually take Maddox places. That's the problem.

That's going to change. He needs to become my priority.

He's given me everything I've ever wanted, and it's time I do the same for him.

"Dude," Maddox says breathlessly and stills with my cock

still buried deep inside him. "I'm giving you my best work here, and you're off in fairyland."

"Did you just call me a fairy?"

He's unamused. "Fuck off. What are you thinking about?"

My thumb traces his bottom lip I so desperately want to kiss. "I've been so unfair to you all these years."

"What?" He pants, trying to catch his breath.

"I promised you a long time ago that we'd see the world together, and then all I've done since then is work."

"We have forever. And need I remind you, we're in Fiji. We can't expect to see the entire world in only a few years. Reality comes first. Which means responsibility and *work*."

"I love you so much, and I don't want you to lose your impulsive side. It's what made you take a chance on me even though you'd never been with a man before. I'm going to do better."

Maddox smiles. "The only way you could do better right now is if you go back to fucking me and stop worrying about making me happy. I *am* happy."

I roll my hips and move inside him, and he throws his head back with a groan. His long neck is exposed, and I waste no time nipping at it, while I reach between us and stroke his cock.

"Like this?" I murmur against his skin.

"Uh-huh." He rises up onto his knees and sinks down on me and then does it again, slowly fucking himself on my dick.

"I love you," I say again.

"I love you too. Always."

I grip his hips hard and meet his thrusts until we're breathless and panting.

"Damon." Maddox grunts as he comes. He trembles in my

arms, while his cum coats us both, and I pull him closer, holding him tight through the aftershocks.

He nods into my neck, giving me permission to keep going.

"Hold on to the headboard because this is gonna get rough."

Maddox reaches behind me. "Bring it."

It doesn't take long for me to reach breaking point and come inside him.

When our breathing evens out and he climbs off my lap, I slink down into the crisp sheets and land my head on the fluffy pillow as I watch him make his way to the bathroom. We started going without condoms when we moved in together, and no matter how many times I see it, I can't help loving to watch my cum dripping down his legs when he moves to get cleaned up. It's my little way of claiming him.

Before he reaches the bathroom, Maddox looks over his shoulder. "You're watching again, aren't you, caveman?"

No point in denying it. "Yup."

"You're sick."

"You say that, but you really love it."

The shower starts, and I figure I have just enough time to get out my phone and rearrange some shit in our schedules. I wasn't lying when I said I was going to do better.

I'm thankful Maddox takes long showers, because it takes a while to make some calls.

I'm tying up the last loose end when Maddox comes back into the room wearing only a towel.

"Seriously? You couldn't even get up to wipe yourself down? Lazy-ass."

I grin. "Seriously? You're taking that tone with me even

though I just spent twenty minutes planning a way for us to extend our trip and go to Australia like you originally wanted?"

Maddox's usual happy and relaxed face turns stoic. "You what?"

"I was serious, Maddy. You deserve everything, and I'm going to find a way to make my job a second priority from now on. I've been going full speed for four years, and I should be stable enough to take more time off. I mean, I'll still have my phone on, and I have to work remotely if something with one of my players pops up, but—"

Maddox's smile is brighter than it's been in a long while. "Really? I mean … you're serious? We're going to Australia?"

"On one condition."

"What's that?"

"We don't go hiking while we're there. Poisonous plants everywhere. I won't even mention the animals."

Maddox runs and jumps on the bed, losing the towel and climbing on top of me again. "Deal."

CHAPTER THIRTEEN

MADDOX

Damon refuses to marry me but is still wearing my ring.

This shouldn't make me so damn happy, but it does.

He gets me. He understands me.

He knows I was proposing for him.

Then, on top of not marrying me, he's extending our trip. *For me.*

I know he wants to travel more and do more things with me, but his career is important, and it's hard for him to avoid his responsibilities. He's not as carefree as I am.

We spend the rest of the morning researching stuff we can do while we're in Australia, but that's interrupted when we get an incoming video chat from Stacy.

"Can I please, please, please fuck with her?" I ask.

Damon laughs. "And say what? That I turned down your proposal? Oh wait …"

"Ooh yeah. She's so going to think we're lying." *I can't wait.*

"Are you two ever going to grow up?"

"Nope." I shove him out of view and hit the Answer button while trying to keep my face disappointed-looking.

Her bright eyes fill the screen. "Hey, soon-to-be … wait." Stacy frowns. "You chickened out, didn't you?"

"You're not going to believe what happened. So, we were hiking, right—"

"Where is Damon? He can't hear this?"

"No, he's with Matt and Noah."

Damon glares at me. Probably for lying so well. But eh.

"Anyway, I had it all planned out and was giving myself a pep talk when I fell over and totally pierced my hand on a poisonous plant. I was crying, 'God no! Why? Lord, why would you take me from the love of my life when I was about to propose?'" I'm totally nailing this dramatic reenactment. "So then your brother was all, 'Wait, proposal?' and I said, 'Dude, I'm dying here,' and he said 'I don't care. Where's my ring, bitch?' and so I decided not to do it and we broke up."

"Great story. Now tell me the truth."

"Hey!" I protest. "Most of that was true, but it was Damon who thought I was dying and me trying to give him the ring, but he said no."

She makes a buzzer noise like from a game show. "Try again. He would not say no to you."

"He did!"

"Uh-huh. When's the wedding?"

I grunt and turn to Damon. "Babe, help."

"Hey, you wanted to fuck with her. You have to convince her you're not lying now."

"That right there is why we're not getting married." I turn to my best friend. "This isn't like the time you spent a week on a cruise with my friend from high school and then you ran off

105

to Pennsylvania to marry him and have his babies like the big practical joke that it is."

She rolls her eyes. "Yes, I'm playing the long game with this con. Giving up New York, moving to the sticks, and birthing twins is my master plan for the ultimate joke. When the girls turn eighteen, I'm going to turn around and say, 'Ha! Gotcha!'"

"I knew it!" I exclaim. "No one would voluntarily have ginger-headed kids."

Jared's voice comes through the speakers. "Heard that, asshole. You know they're practically your nieces."

"Miss you, you soul-sucking redhead. Miss your spawn even more though."

Truthfully, I couldn't be happier for Stacy. She's become an entirely different person since leaving the city and falling in love with a really great guy. I might be biased considering he's my childhood friend, but whatever.

Damon moves closer and wraps his arm around me while staring into Stacy's confused gaze. "I really did say no to him."

"What?" she shrieks. "Why?"

"Because we're practically already married and no piece of paper will change that?"

"But—"

"Stace." Damon puts on his big-brother voice. "I'm happier than I've ever been in my entire life. That's all that matters."

"Okay." Her lips purse. "Happy non-engagement? I guess."

"Thanks." I grin. "We've been celebrating not getting married *all* morning."

She winces. "Still don't need to know those details."

"Momma, milk," an adorable little voice says behind her.

Stacy rolls her eyes. "No milk. Bed."

It's way past the twins' bedtime.

"Milk."

"Bed."

"Milk!"

She glances back at us. "I have to go. Non-congrats again."

The screen goes black.

"Thank fuck you don't want kids," Damon says. "The twins are adorable but—"

"No, thanks."

"Exactly." Damon kisses the side of my head. "I knew you were the perfect man for me the moment I laid eyes on you."

"Liar. I know your exact thoughts of me when we first met."

"Oh?"

"Yup. It was 'This straight guy with his gorgeous blue eyes and blinding smile is an asshole."

Damon laughs. "That's actually disturbingly accurate."

"It's because I totally am the perfect guy for you, but it took you longer than me to see it."

"What are we gonna tell the guys?" Damon asks.

"That I'm way smarter than you because I worked out we were soul mates before you even wanted to fuck me?"

"About the non-engagement, dumbass."

"It's not nice to call your soul mate a dumbass."

"Dearest soul mate, love of my life, not my future husband … what are we going to tell the guys?"

I shrug. "Whatever you want to tell them. Nothing sounds good. How about nothing?"

"Stacy was the only one who knew your plan?"

"And my parents."

Damon nods. "I'm good with nothing, then."

Only, someone gets distracted all afternoon—definitely not my fault—and by the time dinner rolls around, Damon forgets he's still wearing the ring.

So when Damon stands and raises his glass to toast Matt and Noah's announcement that they're going to have a baby, Noah's gaze catches on Damon's hand.

"What the fuck is that?"

Damon's eyes widen. "Shit."

With a sigh and a smile, I stand. It doesn't matter to me if the guys find out, but explaining it a million times over is what I wanted to avoid. Damon and I understand it, but I know others won't. At least everyone's here at the same time so we don't have to repeat it—a rare feat for our group lately. "We have an announcement as well."

Damon and I stare at each other, and then together, we say, "We're *not* getting married!"

And yep, as predicted, we have to explain it to all the confused faces in the room. That only seems to confuse them more.

"So no wedding, but you're going to live like husbands?" Miller asks.

"Exactly."

Miller turns to Talon. "Maybe we should do that."

"No wedding?" Talon exclaims. "No way. We're doing it and selling the pics for a shit ton of money."

"Like we need more money?"

While they argue over their upcoming nuptials, Damon and I share a look. One that says we definitely made the right decision, because who wants to deal with wedding venues and catering and everything else that comes with planning a wedding? I shudder. No, thanks.

They talk details, while Damon and I share our own toast.

"To not getting married," he whispers in my ear.

"Amen."

We click our glasses together and take a sip, but then Noah catches my eye.

He throws his arm around Lennon. "So, Beatle. Matt and I are raising babies. Maddox and Damon are *not* getting married, but kinda are, but not really. Talon and Miller are walking down the aisle. What are you and Ollie gonna do?"

Ooooh, if looks could kill, Matt would be a widower.

Everyone at the table blinks and does that awkward thing where we know we should look away but can't wait for the train wreck we see coming.

Ollie and Lennon's mouths hang open, but nothing comes out.

Noah grins. "Did I put you guys into a pressure cooker and set it on high?"

Fucking Noah, the shit stirrer.

Lennon breaks first. "You're so ready to be a parent."

He escapes an answer by going the sarcasm route, but I think everyone can see the question floating around in both their heads.

All I can say is good luck to them, and I hope they know what they both want.

I will be forever grateful for finding maybe the one singular person in the world who understands me even better than myself.

I'm never letting Damon go.

III

OLLIE AND LENNON

CHAPTER FOURTEEN

Nothing puts your relationship under a microscope faster than everyone around you taking giant steps forward.

Noah and Matt are going to be parents, Talon and Miller are getting married, and Damon and Maddox are … well, they're staying Damon and Maddox.

It works for them.

What Lennon and I have has been working for us.

I'm happy. *So happy.*

Then why is there something in the back of my mind telling me that I *shouldn't* be happy and content with what we have? That I should want more.

In the last three years, we've been there for each other while we've both gone through a lot in our professional lives.

Lennon gave up his dream job of working for *Sports Illustrated* to take a shitty media position with my team so he could be with me. That only lasted one hockey season before he was re-offered his dream job but for a position where he could be based out of New York. He also still has his running feature of queer athletes for the magazine and has been killing it. With more and more athletes slowly coming out of closets, he has a steady stream of articles to write.

He's even been headhunted to audition for on-air positions with different networks, but he hates public speaking and keeps turning them down.

Meanwhile, I've worked my way from being a player with one of the highest assist records in the league to being one of the highest scorers. I'm becoming invaluable, and Stanley Cup whispers have been happening for the last three seasons. We've made the playoffs every year since I was traded to the team.

And yeah, it probably has a lot to do with teamwork and trust on the ice, not my trade, but try telling that to my superstitious teammates. They're convinced I'm New York's good-luck charm, and hey, I'm not going to fight that kind of praise.

I'm a gay man on an NHL team, and I'm *respected.*

Lennon and I are excelling in all aspects of our lives, so it's not surprising that I'm disgustingly happy. I'm so happy I feel guilty when I hang around Soren because his life is a mess right now.

Yet, Noah has managed to create this tense vibe with one simple question.

It feels like I'm on a third date and I'm being asked "Where is this going?" even though it's Lennon and we've been together for three years, not three dates.

When Lennon leans in closer to me and asks if I'm ready to go to bed, I almost want to say no. Because with Noah's taunt in the air, I get the feeling we're headed for a long discussion about something I have no idea about.

Which makes me wonder if this is something I should have

been thinking about the past three years.

We've spoken about the future, have maybe mentioned marriage in passing, but we've always said our careers are more important and that it would be a future discussion.

I haven't really thought about it since.

When my ex, Ash, got engaged and married to my brother a year ago, my only thought was I'm happy Ash got everything he ever wanted. Lennon didn't enter the equation or thought process.

I thought it was because I've been so secure in Lennon's and my relationship and where we were that marriage didn't need to be a part of it. Of us.

What does it say about me that I don't want to marry my boyfriend?

"Ollie?" Lennon frowns at me.

"What?"

"I asked if you were ready to go."

Oh. Right. That.

I nod stiffly. "Sure."

We say goodnight to the guys, and as soon as we leave the dining hut, it's a reflex to take Lennon's hand.

We're comfortable and easy.

Wow, so romantic, Ollie.

The evening Fijian breeze hits us as we walk to our side of the island. The bright moonlight glints off the calm water lapping at the shore.

Lennon shivers, and I wrap my arm around him—another reflex.

We may be comfortable and easy, but everything about us feels *right*.

So how can that be a bad thing?

"What are you thinking about?" Lennon asks.

Here we go.

"Thinking about how you'll owe me twenty bucks by the time this vacation's over," I lie. It's not that I haven't been thinking about the little bet we made years ago, but I'm not thinking about that right now.

"Uh, for all the sex we're having?" Lennon asks. "That's pretty cheap, but I approve. Although, if things with the NHL don't work out, you might have to up your rates when you sell your body on the street."

See, that's why I love him. He makes me laugh. Every. Damn. Day.

"I'll keep that in mind, but I actually mean about Jet and Soren."

Jet and Soren have side-by-side cabins, and the second I realized that, I knew it was either brilliant or stupid.

Noah and Matt have the biggest suite which even has its own private beach at the most northern point of the island. The rest of the cabins are spread around. Damon and Maddox's is right near ours.

Putting the two single guys together is good because they don't have to listen to the copious amount of sex that's going on with the couples. But it could also be stupid because I swear something happened between Jet and Soren years ago. Lennon thinks I read way too much into the fleeting glances between them.

"That bet was for something happening between them three years ago. Not now," Lennon says.

"Uh-huh, so you totally think they're gonna hook up."

Lennon sighs. "I'll miss Soren when Matt and Noah kill him."

I laugh, but my boyfriend turns serious.

"Is that all you're thinking about?"

Lennon reads me so well I'm not surprised he knows that's not all, so I get it over with.

"Noah's a dick, huh?"

Lennon pushes his glasses back up his nose. I love those glasses. Without them, Lennon's hot, no doubt, but with them? He's like the epitome of the nerdy-geek fantasy, and I might have a fetish.

"Oh, honey, if you're only now working out Noah's a dick, I'm going to start feeling bad about all the dumb jokes I make about you. It's one thing to say it when you know it's not true. It's really mean if you are that slow."

I hip-check him. "Funny, nerd."

"What'd Noah do this time?"

I'm surprised he doesn't automatically know, which makes me pause. Maybe Noah's taunt only made *me* rethink things.

I stop walking and pull Lennon to face me. His gorgeous face is passive and giving away nothing. Guess I'm not as good at reading my boyfriend as he is at reading me.

"Did I miss something?" he asks.

"The whole pressure cooker comment."

Lennon waves me off. "That? Wouldn't be Noah without a little shit stirring. It's not even worth thinking about."

"Our future isn't worth thinking about?"

He cocks his head. "Is that what I said?"

"Basically," I mutter.

"Okay, what's up? Are you trying to pick a fight or something?"

"No." Yes. Maybe.

"Noah's words are not worth thinking about because he was trying to get a reaction out of us," Lennon says.

"I guess with all the proposals and weddings and babies, I thought he had a point."

"He did?"

Okay, so an hour ago, I would've said no, but now … "Guess not. If you're happy, I'm happy."

Lennon scoffs. "That sounds convincing."

I throw up my hands. "Well, shit, I don't know. Do you ever think about that stuff?"

"Marriage and kids? Not really."

"You don't think about our future?"

"Our future, sure. But more along the lines of, what happens if Ollie's traded next season? What happens if I ever get the balls to accept one of those on-air auditions?"

I'm confused. "I thought you weren't interested in them."

"I'm not, but not because I don't want to do it. It's because I don't think I *can*."

I hate when Lennon questions himself and his amazing journalistic talent. He has a way of seeing things in the game that other people don't. And it doesn't matter which sport he's watching. Football, baseball, or hockey. He's knowledgeable in all of them. He can sense tension between teammates, if someone's covering an injury, and he can spot every single mistake a player makes. Nothing gets by him.

Which is why he'd make a great sportscaster. But whenever it's come up, he has always turned it down immediately, saying he'd be a nervous wreck on-screen and that won't make for good sports.

"You know my opinion on that," I say.

"Yeah, that I should go for it even though it'd be a disaster and you would get to mock me endlessly for being a stuttering idiot on YouTube. You want me to become a viral meme."

"Nah, that'd just be a bonus."

Lennon smiles.

"Do you think you'll ever get the balls to say yes?"

"Maybe if the right offer came along. Like, in New York, more money than I'm earning now, flexibility for during the hockey season when I want to sneak into your hotel room during away games."

Well, technically, I leave the hotel and sneak into his, but that's not his point.

"And what happens if I'm traded in your vision of the future?" I ask.

"I can do my *out athletes* articles from anywhere."

That doesn't answer me. Ever since he turned down his original offer from *Sports Illustrated*, I've felt guilty while still enjoying the benefits of having Lennon in the same city as me. It worked out because he ended up being offered a full-time job with them anyway, but I've had a boyfriend who sacrificed a lot for me in the past, and maybe I'm worried that Lennon is making the same mistakes Ash made.

I don't want someone to put their future on hold for me when I don't even know what I want.

Lennon is someone I want in my life forever—that's not what I'm questioning. I want to be with him as long as he'll put up with me, but … what if what I have to give isn't enough?

"Don't you want more?" I ask. "Like, if you listed your top three goals for the rest of your life, what would they be?"

Lennon doesn't even hesitate. "You, an on-air position, and Chris Hemsworth."

"Hmm, do we get to share Chris?"

"Of course. What's mine is yours."

"Seriously though. What would that third thing be?" I hold my breath while I wait for the answer, which doesn't come as fast.

In fact, he hesitates awhile.

"Happiness," he finally says.

"How vague of you."

"Ollie, if you're asking me if I want marriage and kids just hoping I give you the answer you want, that's not going to happen. My opinion on the issue isn't one way or another. Do I think about having kids? Not really. That's probably in the no basket for me because I had a hard time growing up with bullies, and I don't think I could handle seeing my child go through that. Does that mean I wouldn't consider having kids if you wanted them? For you, I'll consider anything. Kids aren't a deal breaker for me either way. Marriage is pretty much the same deal. I've definitely thought about it, but I don't need it to be *happy*."

"Tell me what you need to be happy, because your answer is still vague."

Lennon takes my hands and looks up into my eyes. "Happiness is what we make it, and I don't think we need to meet certain criteria society deems as accomplishments to achieve it."

Fucking hell. How do I get to be with this guy? What good deed did I do in a past life to have someone so perfect in this one?

"I love you so fucking much," I say.

Lennon grins. "Hey, look at that. You're acing this making me happy thing with three little words."

"Now who's the dumb one? That was six words."

I love the sound of Lennon's laugh.

"Are we good now?" Lennon asks.

While I should be relieved, ecstatic, and hopeful that Lennon and I seem to be on the same page about marriage, something still niggles at me, but I don't know what it is. Lack of growth, maybe? Lack of change?

The annoying sense that Lennon and I should be moving forward in some way hasn't gone away, but how do I tell him I still think we need more but don't know what that *more* could be?

I push that to the back of my mind for now. "I'm thinking the only way to end this discussion is with blowjobs or something."

Lennon sighs dramatically. "You ask so much of me."

Before I can sass back, his hand fists my shirt, and he pulls me off the path and toward the beach.

"Out here?" I ask.

"Well, it's no childhood treehouse, but we do have the entire island to ourselves."

"Minus eight other guys and the owners," I point out.

Lennon cocks his head. "By the sounds of things, you're feeling a little uncertain about us, so maybe I should spice things up. Voyeurism kink? I could be into that."

"Wait, really?"

"Okay, maybe not so much the being watched part, but the risk of being caught sounds hot."

"Yeah?" I reach for Lennon's waist and pull him close. "In that case, how about you be the one to get down on your knees?"

"I'm good either way, but are you all right with possibly getting caught with your cock out?"

"First, I have my dick out in front of guys every day at work—"

"Lucky them." Lennon reaches for the button on my shorts.

"And second, with the way you know how to deep-throat, I have full confidence no one will be able to see my cock."

"No pressure."

"None at all. I know how good your mouth is." I put my hand on his shoulder, arrogantly pushing him down to his knees as I lean back against a palm tree.

Despite my confident front, I am a little paranoid about the other guys catching us.

The little assurance I have is everyone is still at dinner, and even if they weren't, the only two who would come this way are Damon and Maddox.

The small risk adds in a little adrenaline.

Lennon doesn't even tease me a little first, which makes me think he's just as anxious and nervous to not get caught.

As soon as my fly's undone and my cock is out, it's engulfed by his warm and talented mouth.

Jesus, that mouth.

Lennon may have confidence issues when it comes to his career, but one place he's never lacked ego is in the bedroom. He knows how to get me off and get me off fast. He's certain of his own limits as well as mine. He's not shy about exploring or telling me what he doesn't like.

After three years together, I thought we knew all there was to know about each other sexually, but it never ceases to amaze me that I can't get enough of it. Enough of him.

He continues to suck me, and those damn glasses begin to slip down his nose.

I love the sight of him on his knees, driving me crazy, but I'd love it equally as much if he was the one staring down at me while I worked him over.

"Fuck, Lennon," I rasp.

He grunts an acknowledgment but doesn't stop.

My orgasm builds with every wet pull on my hard shaft. Lennon's mouth doesn't let up, doesn't give me a chance to breathe.

Shallow panting fills the night air, my back rubs against the rough side of the palm tree, and my muscles contract and tighten, winding to the point I'm about to explode.

My balls draw up, preparing to let go of everything I have. Just … need … one more … second—

"What're you guys doing?" Maddox's knowing taunt cuts through the dark.

But it's too late. I'm coming.

Lennon pulls away, and I turn toward the beach so Maddox and Damon can't see me come all over the ground.

I have to bite my lip to stop any sound from escaping. There's nothing I can do to stop as cum keeps spurting out of my cock. I grip the base of my dick and will it to hurry the fuck up and empty, all the while trying not to pass out from the pleasure rocking my whole body.

Lennon stands. "Uh … Ollie got something in his foot. I was … uh … checking it out."

Both Damon and Maddox laugh.

Fuck.

"Uh-huh. Sure," Maddox says. "If it makes you feel any better, we've already checked. No poisonous plants in Fiji."

"Thanks," Lennon says.

"Definitely none where you need to suck the poison out," Damon says.

Fuck, fuck, fuck.

"Definitely not the way Lennon was doing it anyway."

"Shit," Lennon hisses.

I still can't talk.

With nothing to wipe myself with, I put my dick back in my shorts and do them back up. When I turn, I casually lean against the tree with my cum-covered hand and subtly—at least I hope to fucking God it's subtle—wipe it on the bark.

I can only see Maddox and Damon's silhouettes in the dark. "What's up?" I play dumb. I'm good at it. Just ask Lennon.

They laugh again.

"Have a good night, guys," Damon says and pushes Maddox along.

"We don't get to mock them more?"

"No. Soren let the plane thing with us go, so we should be bigger people and let this go."

"What happened on the plane?" I call out.

"If we tell you, we get to mock you," Maddox says.

"Pass," Lennon cuts in. "Goodnight, guys."

As soon as they're gone farther up the path, Lennon and I let out a collective breath.

"So … getting caught? Not as fun as I thought it would be," Lennon says. "But also, in my head, whoever caught us would be totally hot and someone we don't know and they'd offer to join us."

"And they'd look like Chris Hemsworth?" I ask.

"Of course."

"If I was ever okay with sharing you, I'd let you have your fantasy, but don't hold your breath, because you're mine."
Forever, my mind thinks.

"Could you imagine me with more than one guy? I think my inner teenage nerd would have a stroke before any of the good stuff could happen."

"Accurate."

Lennon loops his arm in mine, and we make our way back to our hut with absolutely nothing changed between us.

And I couldn't be happier.

CHAPTER FIFTEEN

LENNON

Ollie, an on-air position, and happiness.

I truly believe that's all I need. But I'd be lying if I said our conversation didn't keep replaying in my head on a loop.

We keep busy by hanging out with the guys and watching Jet and Soren's epic love story begin in front of our eyes.

The most surprising thing about that is Soren's still breathing.

Guess Matt doesn't want to go to prison for murder seeing as he's about to be a dad.

We spend our days exploring Fiji. We drink, we laugh, and we all endure the obligatory ribbing that always happens when our group is together.

At least Maddox and Damon keep their promise and don't tell everyone what they caught Ollie and me doing. Otherwise, it would be endless mocking.

So far, we've been relatively unscathed apart from Noah's singular taunt about what the future holds for Ollie and me.

Which brings me back to my boyfriend's mini freak-out the other night.

I lie awake, staring at the wood ceiling of our luxury hut, trying not to think about what would've happened if I was the type of guy to want marriage.

If one question can rattle Ollie's confidence in what we have, that can't be a good thing.

He stirs beside me, curling into my side and then continuing a light snore.

I don't want to do anything today but this.

I want to hold my loveable giant in my arms and remind him of what we have. It's not so much a need to prove our love, but a desire to show him that he shouldn't ever have to worry about us. We're solid.

The only time I've ever thought about marriage with Ollie is when his ma gives us her look. Oh, yeah, she has a look. A stern one that she covers with a smile.

She has already thrown two weddings for her sons, one a same-sex wedding, so I don't know why she's pushing for her other three to get hitched too. News flash, Ma Strömberg: marriage doesn't always equal happily ever afters.

Take my parents, who after twenty-eight years together filed for divorce the second my little sister graduated from college.

Vows of forever aren't appealing to me when you have a back-out clause attached.

I want to do something for Ollie to show him how committed I am to us no matter what. If in a few years he decides he has to be a father, I could live with that. It's doubtful that'll happen with his brothers giving him a billion nieces and nephews to dote on instead, but if he wants it, I'll give it to him. I'll give him anything he wants.

Even marriage.

I just don't *need* these things.

All I want is Ollie's support, to get over my stage fright and move forward in my career, and above all, to be happy.

Whatever that might entail.

It's hard to know how to *show* that though without some big declaration of love like a marriage proposal.

I'm still thinking about it when Ollie wakes properly.

He trails his lips up my shoulder and buries his head in my neck. His blond hair tickles my nose.

Ollie's large hand runs down my side and grips my hip to roll me toward him.

Our naked bodies fit perfectly together—always have—and as much as I want to continue this …

I roll away from him and out of bed. "As much as my cock wants you, I have to take a leak. I've been waiting for you to wake up."

Ollie chuckles but follows me into the bathroom.

"I don't need any help. Thanks though."

My boyfriend laughs again and gets in the shower.

He's not much of a talker in the morning.

After I piss, I reach to flush the toilet, but Ollie's gruff voice stops me.

"Don't even dare."

I smirk and press it, stealing cold water from the shower, and he screeches as he jumps away from the spray.

Then he crooks a finger at me. "Get your ass in here."

"Why? You gonna spank it? Voyeurism kink, spanking … This vacation has been enlightening."

"Get your butt in here, will you?"

Reluctantly, I do and await a punishment that doesn't come.

Instead, Ollie pulls me close and wraps his arms around me. "We got plans for the day?"

"Don't think so. Everyone's doing their own thing. What'd you have in mind?"

He turns us and presses me against the tile. Warm water beats down on us, getting him more so than me, and I shiver from the cold at my back.

"I have a really great idea." Ollie's using his sex voice, and my dick is fully on board.

"Let me guess, it has something to do with getting dirty before we get clean?"

Ollie's hand moves down my side, over my ass, and grips my thigh so I wrap my leg around his waist. He lowers his head, his lips meeting mine hard. His tongue ravishes my mouth.

I cannot get enough of this man, and I don't think I ever will.

Our lower halves grind against one another while I mentally beg Ollie to reach for my cock. It's hard and needy.

We don't have telepathy—clearly—because instead of doing what I want, his fingers tease my balls and then inch closer to his favorite spot. Mine too. His middle finger circles my rim, and I let out a loud, begging breath, but where I expect him to push inside, he pulls back with a laugh.

"Actually, I was thinking something else."

Ollie ducks his head under the water and rinses off, leaving me breathing heavy and confused as to what just happened.

"You're fucking edging me?" I grumble.

"Punishment for stealing my water. Plus, you know you love it."

"Not right now, I don't."

"You will later."

"Like, as soon as we're out of the shower?" My tone is way too full of hope for Ollie to agree to that.

"Nope."

Damn it.

"Get cleaned up and meet me in bed." With a kiss to the top of my head, Ollie gets out of the shower and dries off.

I rush through the rest of my shower but make sure to clean *everywhere.*

Only, when I'm done and walk back into our room completely naked, Ollie's fully dressed on the bed with his laptop open.

"I get it. It's your plan to blue-ball me all day," I say.

"Maybe. Depends on how bored I get watching this." He spins the laptop to face where I'm standing, and the browser's open to the official Major League Baseball site.

"I'm confused."

Ollie shrugs. "I know how much you love baseball, and you've been missing out since being here. We have nothing to do today, so …"

"We're in Fiji. Shouldn't we do Fiji things?"

"You were willing to spend the day in bed having sex. What's the difference?"

"Uh, both of us will enjoy sex. You don't like baseball."

"I like baseball enough. I just can't follow it."

I snort. "How hard is it to follow? Hit the ball and run."

"Yeah, but then there's things like double plays—"

"When there's two outs on the one play."

"And, like, fly ball, pop ball, line drive … It's too much for my small hockey-orientated brain. You know it can't hold a lot of information."

I have no idea what Ollie's up to, but I go with it and climb on the bed next to him while refusing to put any clothes on. I grab my glasses from the bedside table and slide them on.

"You're not even gonna go with shorts or something?" Ollie asks, eyeing my naked form.

"Nope. If you're going to tease me, you need to be punished as well."

"Brave move, but if you insist." Ollie clicks on the Blue Jays versus Yankees game to live stream it.

It's a slow game, neither team on the scoreboard yet. The Yankees get a shot with loaded bases and only one out, but the Blue Jays' pitcher pulls through under pressure and strikes out the next two batters.

Every now and then Ollie will ask a question as if he's genuinely interested in the answer, which he's never done before.

Usually when I watch baseball, he'll play games on his phone or go for a workout. He leaves me to watch my first love in peace.

So this is weird.

But I put it down to maybe him trying to bond more, or maybe this is his big grand gesture seeing as proposals are off the table.

I will commit my life to you and prove it by enduring baseball.

It's not exactly the type of gesture I've been thinking, but also, I have no fucking clue what I could do for him, so at least he's making an effort.

I'm still at square one.

I could show him how much I love him with sex, but that's not really the kind of declaration I'm looking for. Plus, by the look of it, he's not that interested. Or he's trying not to be.

He's avoiding eye contact with my lower half and focusing way too hard on a game he doesn't even like.

"Why are you acting weird?" I ask.

"Weird? I'm not acting weird, am I?" He doesn't take his gaze off the screen. "Okay, I don't understand this whole stealing bases thing. It's like cheating."

Normally, I'd laugh, but instead, I'm more interested in what he'll do if I move my hand down and give my cock a hard pump.

Ollie glances at it for half a second before focusing back on the game. "Whatcha doing?"

"Baking a cake. What're you doing?"

"Wondering why you're doing … that instead of watching baseball."

"Doing what?" I give my cock another stroke.

"Lennon," he warns.

"Remember the first time we were kinda together but not because we weren't allowed to touch?"

His Adam's apple bounces. "Uh-huh."

"Remember how hot that was?"

"Baseball," Ollie blurts.

My hand stills, and I tilt my head toward him. "What?"

He clears his throat. "We should be watching baseball."

"Jerking off sounds more fun." I really want to ask what

he's playing at, but it's clear he isn't going to tell me without a little incentive.

I go back to stroking myself and use my free hand to reach down and squeeze my sac. I throw my head back and moan as I go from lazily playing with my cock to pulling on it until the tingle of an impending orgasm fills my balls.

"Fuck it," Ollie hisses. He reaches for his phone and hits a button, then takes the laptop and places it next to the bed.

It takes me a second to register the phone thing.

"Wait, what did you just do on your phone?" I ask, my hands stalling.

"Nothing. I'll tell you later."

"Uh, no, you will tell me right now. Or the show stops." To prove my point, I stop touching myself completely and hold my hands up.

"Ugh. Fine." Ollie takes his phone and hits a button.

My voice comes out of the tiny speaker of the phone. "*I get it. It's your plan to blue-ball me all day.*"

"You were recording?" Why in the hell would he do that?

"Only voices. No video. As tempting as it was with this view." Ollie's gaze drops to my crotch again. "But listen." He moves the recording along until we're talking about the game on the laptop.

Our banter—while mostly sexual—is easy and flowing, and I sound like I know what I'm talking about. I mean, I *do* know what I'm talking about, but anytime I've tried to put my thoughts together on purpose, say practicing in front of a mirror for an on-air position, I sound stiff and formal and I develop a stutter which makes me sound unsure.

"You were made to do this," Ollie says. "When you're

relaxed and not thinking, you're funny and have this charismatic charm to the way you speak. Your opinions sound like facts, and I know you can do this."

"Th-that's why you did this?"

"I wanted to show you that if we maybe start slow and practice while you're knowingly being recorded, maybe you could get over some stage fright. We could take it in steps, like maybe start a podcast or something. During the off-season, I could help you commentate on baseball or we can review the last football season or … I don't know, I'm throwing ideas out there."

"You … you want to start a podcast with me. To talk about sports. That aren't your own."

"Well, it'd be a bit biased to critique other hockey teams while I'm still playing. Plus, if I say someone's in a slump, I may as well paint a target on my back on the ice."

I shake my head. "That's not what I meant. You're willing to do this for me just because you know I don't have the balls to do something like this on my own."

Ollie runs a hand through his hair. "Well, uh, yeah. Because I love you, and I want you to have the three most important things in life. Me, your dream job, and happiness. You already put your other dream job on hold once before for me, so I don't see why I shouldn't help you any way I can to get this one."

"Fuck, Ollie."

He frowns. "That sounded whiny. Why are you whiny?"

"Because this … this is more perfect than any wedding vows. More precious than simply saying I love you."

This is the perfect grand gesture, and I've still got nothing.

"I do love you," Ollie says. "More than anything."

"I love you too."

His face lights up. "Good. Can we jerk off together now?"

I laugh. "The most romantic moment of my life ends with *that*."

"That's what you get when you want me for the rest of your life."

"Slight glimpses of romance and offers of handjobs?" Hmm, that actually doesn't sound like the worst thing in the world.

"I put the romance in fucking."

"That sounds like an oxymoron."

"What'd you call me?" Ollie exclaims.

I laugh again. "You're a goofball."

"A goofball who's sexy and hot and is about to jerk off in front of you." Ollie's shirt disappears, his rippling muscles making the tattoos along his arms, shoulders, and chest appear like they're dancing along his skin.

His shorts go next, and he's not wearing any underwear. He must have at least known this is where it was going to end—with us naked again.

"Same rules as the first time we ever did this?" I ask.

"Fuck no. I need to kiss you."

Ollie rolls his big body toward me and leans in.

His mouth captures mine while his hand snakes down to his cock.

I love his tongue, the feel of his big body close to mine, and all I want to do is look down at him and his impressive cock. I love that too.

I love everything about Ollie.

Everything.

As he jerks himself, his hand hits the side of my leg repeatedly, which only turns me on more.

I know if I go anywhere near my dick, I won't last. Not after the way Ollie touched me in the shower, and definitely not after teasing myself to punish him. I always forget teasing leads to more frustration on my part.

Ollie pulls back. "You gonna join in on this?"

I push him onto his back and climb on top of him, straddling his thighs. "I might want to watch you for a bit."

His hazel eyes shine in amusement.

"How long do you think you can last *without* touching yourself?"

"That's so not a challenge I'm going to take right now." I'm achy and needy, and at this point I'm sure I could probably come from watching him.

Especially when his big muscles shudder as he lets out a raspy breath when he continues to stroke himself from tip to root.

Ollie is and always has been my ultimate fantasy. A powerful and masculine jock with a heart of gold.

I can't help admiring him in all his physical glory.

I run a hand over his impressive chest and down his intricate tattoos on his arm. "All of this is mine."

Ollie huffs a laugh but nods. "All yours." His lips remain parted, and I know his tells. I know he's close.

I lean over and kiss him again, just as I reach for my own cock to finish this.

It doesn't take long at all.

Ollie's bucking and grunting while I swallow the deep and guttural sounds he makes. It sends me over the edge until we're both messy and panting.

They say a man's mind is never clearer than after he comes, and as I find the energy to sit back up, my thighs still clinging to Ollie's sweaty skin, the answer to my grand gesture has been right in front of my eyes all along.

And right now, it's painted in cum.

CHAPTER SIXTEEN

OLLIE

L ennon's had a weird smile on his face for *days*.

Granted we haven't been doing much but staying in our hut, waking up late, spending our days on the beach, and finally getting a true vacation.

The first week was crazy with group activities, but now our time in paradise is winding down, we've all split up to do our own thing.

After almost two weeks of allowing myself to relax enough to not want to get back into my strict diet and workout routine, I'm just about ready for home. The bliss of lazing in the sun and eating ten times as many calories as I'm working off has to end sooner or later—the sooner the better or preseason will kill me.

Today, Lennon's taking me to the mainland for a surprise, and I have no idea what it could be. All my guesses of cave tours, shark encounters, and cliff diving get laughed at.

Joni drops us off in Suva, and then we get a taxi to some address Lennon shows the driver on his phone.

Every five minutes I guess something else until my guesses don't even make sense anymore. Like chasing sea turtles to keep as pets. Though, that would be pretty cool. I'd call mine Shelly.

But that's clearly not it when we're moving away from the beach. Plus, you know, it's not legal or whatever.

When the car does finally pull to a stop in a touristy street and we get out, I pause when I see what the plan is. It's hard to miss when it's lit up in neon.

Tattoo.

"Lennon …"

My first thought is Max and Ash would kill me if I got ink from anyone but them. My second thought is that Lennon is buying me a tattoo, and that warms my heart enough to forget about Max and Ash and whatever they might say.

"Before you tell me you can't cheat on your brother and get ink from someone else, I called Max."

My brow scrunches. "You. Called my brother. The brother who's married to my ex-boyfriend. While you are my current boyfriend."

Things between Max, Ash, me, and Lennon have been getting better. We're always civil, but it's still so damn awkward. There's no resentment on any of our parts, but seeing each other only a few times a year helps.

Lennon laughs. "Yes. I called Max. He recommended this place. So …" He gestures for me to go in.

The place looks clean—bonus—and the walls are covered in intricate and difficult designs.

"What are you buying me?" I ask as I look over some Fijian tribal patterns.

"Oh, we're totally using your credit card, Mr. Money Bags."

I smile. "I'm cool with that, but what design? Ooh, a turtle." I run my finger over it.

"No. We have our own designs to get."

My hand drops. "Wait, we?"

The grin that lights up Lennon's face makes my breath catch.

A big guy covered in tribal tattoos appears from a back room. "Ah, you must be Ollie and Lennon. I'm Adi. Who's first?"

"That would be me," Lennon says. "Before I lose my nerve." His chuckle gives away how nervous he is.

"Wait. You're getting a tattoo for me?"

Lennon glances at the guy. "Umm ..."

The guy smiles. "After talking with you about the designs, I figured you two are together. Love is love. Simple as that. You can talk freely. But if you need a minute ..."

"Thanks," Lennon says.

"No worries. Just give me a shout when you're ready."

Lennon slowly approaches, and his face does that thing where he's trying to find the right words. He has it almost constantly while he's writing his articles. "I've been trying to think of a way to show you how grateful I am to have you in my life. We both agreed the other night about what we don't need, but we didn't say what we *do* need. A symbol."

"Matching dildo tattoos?" I joke, because I get the feeling he's freaking out that I won't like this. But I *love* it.

Lennon laughs. "Not dildos. But you'll see. Your brother designed something for us."

"And you're doing this just for me? Even though you've refused to get a tattoo in all the time I've known you."

Knowing he's willing to do this for me—and only me—it's better than anything I could've asked for.

"Nope. I'm doing it for *us*. We may not be wedding people or family people, but this … It's a piece of each other we do have to give."

"You giving me a patch of your virgin skin is the weirdest and most romantic thing anyone's ever done for me."

"Well, when you put it like that, it doesn't sound like the big romantic gesture I thought it was."

I pull him against me. "No, it's perfect."

"You haven't seen the designs yet." He smirks. "Oh, and I forgot to add you won't until they're done."

Minor panic tries to take over, but logically, I know my brother. Ink is his life, and there's no way he'd let someone tattoo something that wouldn't fit his canvas that he and Ash have painted since I was eighteen years old.

So I put on a brave face and pretend I'm not even a tiny bit worried. Which I'm not.

Nope.

Not even a little bit.

Okay, totally a little, but I can handle it.

"Do I get to see yours first?" I ask.

"Maybe after the stencil's applied." He turns and calls out to Adi. "Okay, we're ready."

The big Fijian guy reappears and takes Lennon back, while I wait an excruciatingly long time for a stencil to be put in place.

I end up pacing the small reception area, trying to distract myself by looking at this guy's portfolio.

When they do finally call me in, I walk into the room to find Lennon shirtless on the chair with his left arm above his head.

I round the chair and let out a little laugh, not only at what he's getting but how big it is.

"Go big or go home, right?" Lennon says, his voice shaky.

There on his rib cage is a hockey stick, skate, puck, and the number eighteen. My jersey number. The entire piece is about the size of my hand.

"It'll suck if I ever switch teams and get a new number." That's probably not the first thing I should say when given something this awesome. Oops.

Lennon looks at me through those nerdy glasses of his. "This was your number when we met and when we first got together. I'm keeping it."

"You say that as if tattoos are able to come off with club soda."

"Wait, that's not how tattoos work?"

I try to hide my smile. "Are you sure you want it that big? First tattoo. It's gonna hurt."

"I can take it."

We'll see how long he lasts.

To give him credit, he lasts about an hour before he starts to complain. Which is basically when only the outline is done.

"Shading is gonna be worse," I warn him.

Poor Lennon looks like he's going to vomit.

"Need to take a break?" Adi asks.

My brave boyfriend shakes his head. "No, keep going. Just get it done or I'm worried I won't get it finished."

"Oh, Max would tie you to the chair back home to get it done."

"I don't doubt it," Lennon says.

When his eyes start to water another hour later, I stand by him and grip his hand.

Adi glances up from his work. "You're almost done."

Lennon turns his head toward me. "How have you done this"—he gestures to my tatted body—"that many times?"

"I was Ash and Max's practice. All these pieces have evolved over a few years and many different sessions."

"Your brother is super talented," Adi says. "I didn't believe he was him when he called."

"My brother is famous?" I ask.

"In the world of tattooing? Hell, yeah, he is." Adi takes his gaze off Lennon for a split second to eye my tats. "I can't believe I get to ink his designs on you. Mostly all the requests we get here are touristy things. Cute little turtles and shit."

I'm offended.

When Lennon's finally done and his tattoo is covered with a protective breathable bandage, he gets out of the chair and slides his T-shirt back on with a wince.

Adi changes needles and gets set up for me while Lennon pulls a blindfold out of his back pocket.

"You've been sitting on that this whole time?"

"Uh-huh." He's positively giddy for a guy who's supposedly in pain. "Shirt off."

With a sigh, I take off my shirt and sit in the seat.

Lennon slips on the blindfold.

"Can I request something?" I ask.

"I'm under strict instructions from your brother on what to do and where to put it."

I huff. "Of course. I was wondering if it's a tattoo that could use some color?"

"But none of your tats have color," Lennon says.

I blindly reach my hand out until he takes hold of it. "But this is *your* tattoo. I want color."

"I can do color," Adi says. "But if your brother asks, you forced me, yeah?"

I laugh. "Totally forced you. Twisted your arm."

Lennon keeps hold of my hand while Adi places the stencil on my skin.

It's on my left side, right under my pec along my ribs. It's closer to my heart than where Lennon's was, but it's still in a similar area to his.

The buzz of the tattoo gun isn't anything new to me; neither is the annoying stabbing pain of the needles. I could drift off in this chair.

My tattoo takes half the time of Lennon's, unless I actually do fall asleep, or maybe the blindfold has warped all my sense of time.

Either way, when Adi says he's done and wipes away the blood and cleans me up, nerves sit in the pit of my stomach.

Then I remind myself to trust Max and trust Lennon.

"Are you ready to see it?" my boyfriend asks.

"More than ready." I may or may not be still faking my level of confidence.

You'd think after I got a tattoo with my ex that I'd be scared of going there again, but the thing with my tattoos is they all mean something. My tattoo with Ash represents the four years we had together—the good and the bad times. On one arm I have a Celtic knot tattoo that represents my family. My four brothers and my parents. I have a clock to represent patience and a dove to represent freedom. This new tattoo,

Lennon's representation in my life … it's the most important tattoo I will ever wear.

That's why I asked for it to be in color.

Lennon removes my blindfold, and Adi hands me a small mirror.

A laugh escapes me—a deep, hearty laugh that has a mind of its own.

Because what they chose is so … my family. I'm surprised I didn't guess it.

It's a Superman logo wearing Clark Kent glasses.

"I-is it … o-okay?" Lennon asks.

"Are you kidding me? It's perfect."

"I wasn't so sure with the whole … Superman thing. The glasses, I get. Superman …"

"Lennon." I take his hand. "You may look like Clark Kent, but you're Superman to me. You're selfless and strong. You may not be saving Gotham—"

"Metropolis. God, you can't even nerd properly, jock."

I laugh. "Well, you're my nerd, my Clark … my Superman." I look down at my side again. "This perfectly represents how I see you in my life."

"Better than a wedding certificate and matching rings?"

"I don't need either of those things. We have everything we need right here." I gently place my hand over his bandage.

Lennon's smile is blinding. "You, dream job, and happiness."

"I'll make sure you get it all."

It's one vow I have no problem making.

IV

TALON AND MILLER

CHAPTER SEVENTEEN

MILLER

The sun beats down on my bare skin, the only part not overheating being the small area covered by my tiny boardshorts. Not that I mind.

I'm on an eight point nine-million-dollar yacht anchored off the coast of Fiji, lying back on a deck chair, beer in hand, and Talon and I have everyone at our beck and call.

I can feel Damon's stare without needing to turn my head. "What?"

"When you guys said you were doing your bachelor party here, this is not what I thought we'd be doing."

This is *my* idea of a bachelor party. Relaxed with nothing to do.

Clearly, my fiancé doesn't feel the same way. He's swinging from a rope on the side of the yacht like he's some Tarzan wannabe and cannonballing into the water below.

"Talon asked Joni and Ema about strip clubs. Apparently, Fiji isn't that type of place."

"Eh. This is better anyway." Damon lifts his beer to his lips. "Just not what I expected."

"Yeah, it's all fun and games until your highest-paying client breaks his neck jumping off this boat, and then the NFL will sue your ass and I'll be a widower before we're even married."

Hey, at least then I won't have to tell Talon what I've been keeping from him.

Damon side-eyes me. "Somehow I don't think it'll be the extreme sports that will kill him."

Exactly. "Not gonna think of that while we're on vacation."

"You need to tell him before he finds out from someone else."

I shake my head. "I can't. I just ... can't. You don't understand. This is, like, betrayal to the utmost degree."

"Dramatic much? It's not like you cheated on him."

"I think he'd be quicker to forgive cheating than ... the *R* word."

"You can't even say it, can you?" He leans in closer. "*Retirement.*"

"Shh!" I sit up and twist in the direction where Talon is.

My gorgeous man smiles and waves at me before jumping again.

Good. He didn't hear it.

Damon and I have already decided as a team that my career is done at the end of next season. He's not even going to try to get me another contract.

"Talon will understand. Especially when you tell him your leg's not one hundred percent. He didn't suspect anything when you refused to go wakeboarding the other day?"

Getting out of that one was hard, but claiming to feel

unwell worked out considering I puked everywhere from seasickness later in the day. "Nah. He thought I was sick. Which I was. Technically. But if I tell him I have no faith my leg will hold up, all that's gonna happen is he'll worry and then send me to a ton of different doctors to try to find the one who recommends not retiring and that I'll be fine."

"He will not. Your health comes first. And yeah, you probably do still have a few seasons in you, but you need to think of your future. What if you take one bad hit? He of all people knows sports injuries. Your leg will always be weaker than it had been, and your tear three years ago cut your career by at least twenty percent. Talon would logically know this."

It's my turn to side-eye him. "I'm judging you right now."

"Uh, why?"

"Because you put the words Talon and logic together. Like, in the same sentence."

"How long do you really think you can keep this from him?"

"I don't know. Every time it gets brought up, I could blow him. He likes it when I do that."

Damon laughs. "And when your coaches bring it up in front of everyone in the locker room?"

"If there are any more homophobes lurking on the team, they're gonna get an awesome show."

"Miller—"

"I'll tell him. But not yet. Maybe on the way back into the real world in two days."

Damon reaches over and pats my knee. "Just remember, sooner rather than later. At least before training camp. It's your last season together. Make it worth it."

Worth it.

My whole damn career has been worth it, but the last three seasons being back on the field with Talon have been indescribable. I don't want to leave it behind, but I know my limits. I was lucky to come back after my injury in the first place, and I only have Talon to thank for that.

Keeping it from Talon is idiotic, and sneaking around to doctors behind his back hasn't been easy. But I don't want him to worry, and I don't want him to push for something I've already decided against.

My football career is over. I have one more season left in me, and then I'm done.

A few weeks before coming on this vacation, I used the excuse to go home to see my mom, sister, and niece but instead met with the doctor who did my original surgeries.

After some tests, she assured me my leg is fine and the pinching could be from the nerve damage that both the injury and surgeries caused, but I have to wonder why the pain only started this last season.

Her answer? "It can happen. A physiotherapist will be able to help."

Thanks, Doc. How many years of med school did you go through to come up with that explanation?

According to her, I'm still good. I'm still healthy. I've put a lot of strain on my leg since the injury, but it's holding. For now.

Yet every twinge, every workout, the doubt of it staying that way gets louder and louder.

"Tell him," Damon says and stands. "Preferably before training camp next month. I'm gonna go find Maddy."

I know Damon's right. I just don't want to do it.

Talon and I have achieved our college dream—the ultimate

goal of winning a Super Bowl together. To only last one more season past that does leave a huge sinking feeling in my chest, but we both have to realize that nothing can last forever. Especially NFL careers.

Eight years is an amazing feat. Even if I was only on a practice team for two of those years and out with my injury for one. They still count. Even taking those away, that's still five, and that's more than a lot of players get.

I shouldn't feel ashamed.

But there's still that part of me that remembers what it was like to be injured, watching from the sideline with a broken heart.

Talon and I belong on that field, and I'm giving it up a lot sooner than I expected or wanted, but my gut is telling me it's time.

With Matt and Noah having kids, it's making me think about what Talon's and my future looks like.

Marriage is a given, and I think Talon would make an incredible dad. He'd understand our kids on the most basic level because he's still one himself.

Case in point: with a huge smile, he comes up the side of the boat and appears in front of me dripping wet.

I know what he's going to do before he even makes his move. "Don't even think about it."

He climbs on top of me anyway. "Think about what?"

I grunt. "Doing that."

"Getting you all wet?"

I can't even be mad when he rubs himself all over me. "Do you have to make everything sexual?"

"Have you met me? Besides, this is nothing." Talon grinds his hips while his hand snakes between us to rub my cock over my shorts. One touch from my man and I'm hard and aching for it.

That's what Talon does to me.

"Mm, nothing, huh?" I ask. "Think the other guys would agree if they walked up here right now?"

One of the other guys answers. "Nope. That's downright pornographic."

Ollie.

I didn't even hear anyone come up. It's hard to when Talon's touching me. I guarantee it's how we're going to die. There'll be some big natural disaster, but Talon and I will be too busy fucking to evacuate. Bam. Dead.

Not the worst way to go.

Instead of scrambling off me, Talon teases me more. "You know we like an audience."

Ollie laughs. "I'll pass, thanks. Just came back up here to get a towel. Though, I'm starting to think this group is a little too close for comfort. Soren saw Maddox and Damon going at it, they saw me and Lennon, and now I've seen you two."

"Talon has seen Matt and Noah," I supply helpfully.

"It's the circle of life ... or fucking ... something like that." Talon turns his head toward Ollie. "And if you don't hurry up and get the fuck out of here, you're gonna see a lot more."

Ollie holds up his towel. "I'm out."

Talon flips his hair away from his face, whipping more water all over me. "Now that he's gone ..." He reaches his hand into my shorts now, giving my cock a hard pump.

"Most likely, one of the others will be next."

"Then let them see."

"Or, we could use one of the six bedrooms on this thing and put it to good use."

He lowers his lips to my ear and whispers, "Where's the fun in that?"

"Are you saying sex with me on our own, in a private room, is not fun?"

"Of course not." He climbs off me. "I'll show you."

He helps me up, but as we take the steps to a lower level, the familiar twinge that's been happening on and off since the end of last season makes my leg drop from under me.

Being on the stairs, I tumble, and I'm not small. I try to save myself by gripping the side of the boat, but it doesn't help.

I fall on top of Talon, and we crash to the floor.

"Ouch," Talon says. "But I guess we can do it here." He wriggles beneath me, and as much as I love the feel of his ass rubbing against my cock, I realize it's time.

"Marc?"

At the use of his first name and the seriousness of my tone, Talon loses his trademark joking attitude.

"Fuck, what's wrong?"

"We need to talk." I wince as I get to my feet and grasp the railing of the boat.

"Are you hurt?" Talon jumps up to help me.

I say the words I've been holding on to for months. "It's my leg."

The moment it registers, it's as if I can see Talon's stomach drop.

"How bad is it?" he croaks.

"It'll be fine with some physiotherapy. I saw my surgeon when I went to visit Mom a few weeks back."

Talon frowns. "You went to a doctor and didn't tell me?"

"I didn't want you to worry."

"Well, too fucking bad because I'm fucking worried." His anger is worry, I know that, but this is why I didn't tell him to begin with.

"I'm fine. My leg's good to go for this season."

Talon's lips twist as my words run through his mind.

For this season.

His "Oh fuck" moment is clear on his face. "You're retiring."

I want to protest and deny it, but my mouth won't let the lie pass my lips.

"It's the logical step if you're worried about permanent damage."

I study his face for any of the freaking out I'm expecting, but it's not there.

"Shane, I love you more than anything in this fucking world. More than football. More than *myself*—now, that's saying something. I can't wait to marry you next year and start something new with you. We'll be more of a team than we are now, which means I need to trust your judgment. If you say you're done, you're done."

Wait …

What?

"Who are you and where is my fiancé?" I accuse.

Talon chuckles. "Guess I deserve that. I know I can be pushy, and when you got injured, I might've pushed you a little too hard to get back into it, but I also saw the hunger in you back then. The longing. You weren't ready to say goodbye."

"I'm not exactly ready now," I admit, "but my gut is telling me I have to. I want to have children with you, and I want to be able to actually run after them."

Talon looks … surprised? "You want kids with me?"

"Eventually. What, you don't?"

"No, I do. I've always thought I'd have kids … but I mean, I also thought I'd marry a woman, so I wasn't sure if those plans would change with you or—"

"I want it."

"Me too. And eventually sounds good. Maybe when I'm closer to retirement. I wanna run after them too."

I mockingly gasp. "I can't believe that dirty word came out of your mouth in terms of you doing it."

"Well, I mean, I know I can't still be playing when I'm sixty, but you know … fifty-nine is a good retirement age."

I laugh. "Of course."

Talon pulls me close and wraps his arms around my back. "How does five years sound?"

"What about three? I might be bored by the time five rolls around. Plus, you'll be *thirty-six* if we wait five more years."

"Nope. God and I have a deal. I'm going to stop aging this year. True story."

"Oh, so is this the same deal you made with Him to stop maturing at eighteen too?"

"Exactly." He leans in and kisses the tip of my nose. I kinda love it when he does that. "Kids in three, retire in five?"

"I can work with that, but you know you don't have to retire to have kids. Plenty of the other guys do it."

"They do, but they also complain a fuck ton during the season about missing them. I want to be a present father. Besides, imagining you holding a teeny tiny little baby in your big arms? For that, I'd give football up tomorrow if you asked me."

I pull back. "Look at us being all mature and grown-up and planning our *future*. Our mothers would be so proud."

"Exactly. We play out this next season, we kick ass, and then … wait, what are you gonna do the next three years?"

"I have no fucking clue, but I'm excited for it."

Talon doesn't seem as excited, but I think it might be hitting him that this is it. This is our last season together on the field.

"I'm sorry for telling you during our bachelor party. That's a great way to bring the mood down."

Talon holds me close again. "Oh, my poor, naïve fiancé. If you think this is our actual bachelor party, you're sorely mistaken."

I sigh. "I should've guessed."

"Damn right, you should have. Sometimes it's like you don't know me at all."

CHAPTER EIGHTEEN

TALON

SEVEN MONTHS LATER

There's glitter and boobs everywhere, and it's the best thing ever.

Noah leans closer to yell over the strip club music. "I kinda feel like this is counterintuitive." Says the gay guy getting a lap dance from a woman.

I eye the girl grinding on top of him. "For you guys, maybe. You didn't have to accept the lap dance."

He shrugs. "I always think everyone should experience things at least once."

Miller laughs. "And?"

Noah hands the stripper a crisp fifty to leave. "It's not *horrible*, but … Meh."

"Meh," I scoff. "Meh, he says."

Noah nods toward the other side of the bar. "At least Maddox looks like he's having fun."

We look over toward a semi-private booth with a curtain

half drawn. Maddox sits on Damon's lap while getting a lap dance from one of the strippers.

I laugh. "Fun? He looks like he's in heaven."

When I turn back to Miller and Noah, Miller's got his contemplative stare going on.

"What's wrong?" I ask.

"You want that?"

I know he'd give it to me. It's just a lap dance. But it's too close to our old life—the one where we'd share women and I was oblivious to Miller's feelings.

I don't want to ever make him feel that way again.

There's a difference between wanting something and needing something. I *need* Miller like I need air. Nothing else. Everything else is fun and disposable.

That part of our lives was a huge wake-up call for my denial. Sure, it took a long time for me to figure it out, but it was. It was denial wrapped up in sex. Dangerous combo.

I reach for his hand. "I have everything I need right here. In fact, I want *you* to give me a lap dance."

I try to pull him into my lap, but he's heavy and fairly intoxicated, so he falls to his knees between our seats.

I stare down at him. "This works too."

"I'm kinda scared of what's on this floor."

I laugh and let him up. "Fine. You can give me a lap dance later."

What we have is forever, and next week I get to prove it as we say our vows in front of about five hundred people in some small-town nowhere New York.

The things we're doing to keep this wedding private.

Who's ever heard of *O'Leary* anyway?

"Where's Ollie and Lennon?" I ask.

"They were smart and came up with some bullshit excuse to be late to the lady bar," Noah says.

I purse my lips. "Convenient."

"We're here. We're here." Ollie appears with Lennon behind him.

I narrow my eyes. "Where've you been?"

Lennon's mouth opens. Then closes. "I was ... uh, work meeting."

Ollie rolls his eyes and nudges his boyfriend. "Tell them."

"I ... I ... I'm starting a podcast. A sports one. And ... I was at a vocal coach. Who I've been seeing for the past six months. And she thinks I'm ready to do it. And, and, and ..."

Ollie wraps his arm around Lennon. "And you're going to kill it."

"That's amazing," Miller says.

"It is. You'd be perfect," Noah adds.

Lennon turns to Miller. "I was kinda hoping ... that maybe now you're retired ... that maybe you'd ... y-you'd be interested in doing some podcasts with me. Like as a guest."

"I promise he won't be this stutter-y on the air," Ollie says. "He's just nervous to ask you."

Miller looks at me, and I think we're sharing the same thought. Offers like this are bound to happen. A lot of them he'll want to do. But finding one to fit in with my schedule once the season goes back is going to be hard to find.

"You can do it from Chicago," Lennon says. Maybe we're all sharing the one thought. "We don't have to be in the same room."

I break into a giant smile as Miller's face lights up.

"Then fuck, yeah, I'm in. It sounds awesome." Miller stands and crushes Lennon in a hug.

"We ready to get out of here?" I ask. "Go to a gay bar to satisfy everyone else but the *grooms*?"

Noah doesn't understand I'm being passive-aggressive. That or he's ignoring it. Knowing him, probably the latter. "Yes. Finally!"

Miller hangs back while everyone else goes for the exit. "You cool with the podcast thing?"

"Of course. It sounds perfect."

"Even if I'm going to be professional and totally call you out when you fuck up a play on the field?"

I wouldn't have it any other way, but I'm not going to tell him that. Instead, I'm doing the typical Talon thing. "That's fine by me, because we both know I don't fuck up on the field." I point to myself. "Football legend, remember?"

"Oh, right, sorry. How could I forget?"

In unison, we say the same thing, because he knows what's coming. "Four-time Super Bowl champ, thank you very much."

I pull Miller close and kiss him, because this is the exact reason I'm marrying him. He calls me on my shit, and I love him for it.

CHAPTER NINETEEN

MILLER

The breeze whips by us as Talon directs the rented convertible down narrow and windy roads.

We left all the planning for the wedding to my mom and my sister because if it were up to Talon and me, the theme would be football and all we'd serve is beer and barbecue. It'd be in our backyard and probably not even official because we'd forget to book a legal celebrant.

We had few stipulations for the wedding. It needed to be somewhere relatively secluded and small so the paparazzi wouldn't find us and that we'd get to arrive together. None of this separation the night before crap like traditional weddings. Because let's face it, Talon and I are anything but traditional.

Ironic considering out of all of our friends, we're the only ones having an actual wedding.

Everything else to do with today has been decided by others, and I'm a little worried about what we're gonna walk into.

I have visions of flowers and tulle everywhere.

Yuck.

I stare across at *the Marcus Talon*, still dressed in a T-shirt and jeans because he insists we can throw our tuxes on when we get there instead of being uncomfortable the whole day, and he sends me a smile that's so cocky, so blinding, so … *him*.

I can't believe my best friend from college fell in love with me.

I can't believe we're actually here.

"You nervous?" he asks.

"Nope. You?"

"Well, I do hate being the center of attention, so …"

I bark out a laugh. "I can't wait to call you my husband."

"I prefer the label 'the guy you voluntarily attached your life to because I'm so damn hot and irresistible.'"

"That won't fit on a World's Best mug."

I love that it's so easy between us. I love that he didn't make a big deal out of my retirement or that I don't know what I'm going to do now other than Lennon's podcast.

We'll have kids in a few years, and I want to be home full-time for that, but until then, there's no big plans, and I'm okay with it.

I can tell Talon overthinks for me, but when it comes to careers, he's the serious one out of both of us.

It's uncanny how he can switch from goof-off mode to business mode so easily and frequently, but he's not forcing me to do something—anything—just to fill in my time, and I'm thankful for that.

I'm enjoying having no obligations for once in my life.

When football season starts, I'm probably going to miss it like crazy, but retiring so far has been good for me. I've been able to focus on bigger things, like the fact I'm getting married.

Married.

Talon and I are still smiling at each other when a loud bang makes us flinch.

We swerve on the narrow road, fishtailing and scaring the fuck out of me. Even though he's trying to get the car under control, Talon reaches his hand across me as if to protect me.

If I didn't fear dying right now, I'd mock him about being overprotective. Which in reality just warms my heart that he's thinking of me and my safety first.

I grip onto the armrest and pray we don't flip. Convertibles and rolling cars don't make for great survival stats.

Talon manages to get the car back under control, but it's obvious something's wrong. He pulls off to the side with the telltale sound of a clunking flat following us.

"I think we blew a tire," Talon says.

"Of course we did, because what's a wedding without a little hiccup?"

"Well, let's hope this is the only one."

We get out of the car, and Talon makes his way over to my side where the offending tire is.

I take out my phone. "They got AAA in this town?" Oh. I hold my phone up in the air. "No reception."

"City boy." Talon says this as if he isn't one. Yeah, he grew up in Colorado, but *Denver,* Colorado.

I fold my arms and lean against the car. "This will be fun."

"I'll get this done in five minutes tops."

I grin. "I'll give you ten. If you lose, first blowjob as a married couple is for me."

"I'm pretty sure you can't call sex positions like you do shotgun in a car."

"Hmm, pretty sure I just did."

"Oh, you're so on." Talon gets to work.

Yet, twenty minutes later, he's no closer to changing the tire, and he's a fucking mess.

"I give up." He breathes hard.

"You're also covered in tire grease."

"I may be covered in grease, but after your blowjob, you will be too." Talon tries to come close, but I sidestep him.

"We don't have time. And, I said first blowjob as a *married* couple. We have to actually get to the wedding for that to happen."

"If I have to be all greasy for the wedding, so do you." He boxes me in and cups my face with his dirty hands.

"I hate you."

"Not a nice thing to say to your future husband." Talon continues to cover me in grease by grinding against me. It's all over his shirt and on the legs of his pants from where he tried to wipe his hands.

I should be mad. I want to be mad.

I should care that I'm now as dirty as he is.

But like whenever Talon touches me, is near me, or hell, even looking at me, I get too lost in him to care.

Instead of fighting it, I let it happen.

I let him kiss me, let him press me up against the car, and I don't even stop him when he pulls open the back door and pushes me down on the bench seat.

Talon blankets me with his body. His hips roll, and his hard cock rubs along mine.

I suddenly wish we weren't in public or wearing clothes.

"We're gonna be late to our own wedding," I say in between kisses. "Maybe we should start walking?"

"It's not like they can start without us."

True. "In that case …" I reach between us and pull down his zipper, sneaking my hand inside his boxers and gripping his cock.

"*This* is why I'm marrying you." Talon thrusts into my hand.

"Because I give you orgasms?"

"Nope. Because you're so easily convinced to give me orgasms."

"I'd totally be offended if I could dispute that, but I can't." I stroke him hard and fast, relishing the feel of friction on my own cock through my jeans.

Talon curses and swears like he does when he's getting close.

"Tire grease really turns your crank, huh?" I mock.

"No." He grunts. "It's you. Always you."

"Then give it to me. Come on me. We're gonna have to shower anyway. Somewhere. Do we know if the venue has a shower?"

Talon's hips slow. "Kinda detracting from the point here, Shane."

"Sorry. Right. Coming. Uh, you're coming. You need to come. On me."

"Your dirty talk needs some work. Just shush and let me get there."

A throat clears, and it takes a second to realize the sound isn't coming from either of us.

We still and glance to the side of the road where an officer stands, arms folded like he's trying to look serious, but he has a small smirk on his lips.

"If you want some privacy, might I suggest one of the great hiking trails we have here in O'Leary?"

Talon scrambles off me, pants undone, cock half hanging out.

A small chuckle escapes the cop. "Haven't had to arrest anyone for indecent exposure for about a week. We were due for one, I guess."

"Sorry." Talon tucks himself away. "It's uh, our wedding day, and umm, we should actually be there now, but uh, we got a flat, and, uh …"

I've never seen Talon struggle for words before, so I burst out laughing.

The officer takes off his sunglasses and glances between Talon and me as I sit up. "You're … and you're …"

"Yup," we say at the same time.

He's able to keep any celebrity-awe in check as he goes back to professional mode. "I'm Officer Sloane, but you can call me Silas. Or Si. Or 'Hey, Police Guy' works too. You need a hand with the flat?"

Talon and I glance at each other.

"Oh, uh, we tried—"

"*He* tried," I correct. "And failed. I bet him he couldn't do it. I was, umm, about to collect my win when you snuck up on us."

Officer Sloane scoffs. "Snuck up? You didn't hear my cruiser pull up, the car door close, or me approaching?"

Clearly not.

He shakes his head. "My boyfriend is going to laugh his ass off when I tell him about this."

I begin to panic, because the last thing we need is for this to get out to the public. "Whoa, hang on …"

"No, wait—" Talon starts.

Silas waves us off. "Ev's not going to actually *believe* me. What time do you need to be at the wedding? Half the town is shut down because of it."

I check my phone. "Uh, ceremony is supposed to start in thirty minutes."

"Curse of the Camden Road. Come on, I can take you into town and call Joe."

I frown. "Joe?"

"Tow truck driver. It'll be best if I don't tell him whose car he needs to come and get though. He'll overcharge you."

"Because we're rich?" Talon asks.

"No. Because you betrayed the Pats by signing with Chicago a few years back. He still hasn't forgiven you. He's a massive New England fan."

Talon laughs. "How much will my betrayal set me back?"

"At least double."

"Ooh, steep."

"So, like I said, we won't tell him." He gestures for us to follow him. "Sorry the police cruiser isn't as fancy an entry as that."

We stare back at the bright red convertible.

"Are you kidding me? Talon will love this even more."

Talon bounces on his feet. "Shotgun! And can we put the sirens on?"

Yeah, that sounds about right.

CHAPTER TWENTY

TALON

A rriving with sirens? Fucking awesome.

The commotion catches everyone's attention, and the guests all turn from their seats in the middle of perfectly manicured gardens.

The looks on their faces as we get out of the car are hilarious. Especially Damon's. I think he might be on the brink of having a coronary until we tell him our car broke down and we are not, in fact, under arrest.

"Although only barely," Miller says with a laugh.

We get eyed from head to toe by nearly everyone. Miller and I are dirty, wearing casual clothes, and in no way look ready to be getting married. The ceremony is supposed to start in, like, ten minutes.

So not happening.

Especially when we realize we left our tuxes back in the convertible.

"Tuxes," Miller says, his eyes wide in panic.

Motherfucker.

"Guess we can't get married in our jeans?" I ask. "Ooh, what if we get married in our underwear with just bow ties?"

Miller's mom, Gloria, looks like she could slap me.

"I can go back to the car and bring your tuxes," Officer Silas says.

"Thank you," Gloria says and then turns back to Miller and me. "Why the heck are you two so dirty?"

Silas snorts as he leaves.

"We had a flat tire," Miller says.

Gloria huffs. "Let me go see if we can find somewhere to hose you off."

"Like we're dogs?" I ask.

"There's a bathroom in the room you're supposed to get changed in," Miller's sister says. "It doesn't have a shower, but it has a basin. Come on, I'll show you where to go."

Vanessa leads us to the venue's main building and lets us in a side door.

The room is decorated like a bridal suite with plush lounges and tulle bows everywhere.

"It's in there." Vanessa points. "And I'll go tell the guests why you'll be late if they haven't figured it out already."

"Thank you." Miller goes to hug his sister, but she jumps away.

"Touch me when you're all greasy and I will kill you. Do you know how long it took me to look this good?"

"I can take a guess that it was a really, really, *really* long time," Miller jokes.

Apparently, my fiancé has a death wish. Vanessa can be scary when she wants to be.

Instead of biting back, she tells us to clean up and then storms out.

"You heard her. We should get … clean." I smirk. "Need help getting undressed?"

Miller pulls his stern look that's more adorable than resolute. "You don't think that's gotten us in enough trouble for one day?"

I shake my head. "Wrong. Not nearly enough. It *is* our wedding day. If I don't get to have sex with you, why are we even doing this?"

"To pledge our never-ending love for each other in front of a whole bunch of people we hardly ever see under the pretense that they're important to whatever goes on between you and me."

"Exactly. So why can't we have sex right now?"

Miller thinks about it. Or pretends to. "I guess the car is about fifteen minutes away. It'll be half an hour before Officer Sexy gets back."

"You were checking out the cop?"

"You weren't?"

"I only have eyes for you."

Miller is downright derisive as he says, "Uh-huh."

"Okay, fine. I guess he was good-looking."

"I can't believe you checked someone else out. Rude."

Walked right into that one. I blink up at him as innocently as possible. "You know the only guy to really get my engine going is you."

Miller smiles as he walks into the bathroom, stripping off his shirt as he goes. "You coming?"

"I will be." I chase after him.

I pull out travel lube from my back pocket, and Miller stops with his pants halfway down his thighs.

"Really? Don't remember the tuxes, but you remembered the lube?"

"Priorities." I dribble it on my cock and fingers.

"I thought you owed me a blowjob."

"Decided to fuck you instead."

"You think we have time for you to fuck me?" Miller drops his underwear.

"I will make fucking time," I growl.

Miller's eagerness to go with whatever I say is just one of the reasons I'm marrying him. He braces himself on the small vanity and bends over for me.

"Fuck, I love you." I'm naked and behind him in the blink of an eye.

"Duh."

I nip at his shoulder. Kiss his shoulder blade. My fingers work their way inside his tight ass.

I know I have to be quick, so I might get a little rough scissoring him open.

Miller hisses. "Jesus fuck."

"Too much?"

"No. Keep going." He drops his head against the wall in front of the sink. "Fuck, don't stop."

My hard cock grinds against his ass cheek, getting impatient.

"Do it," Miller breathes. "Do it now."

I remove my fingers and grip his hips as my cock slides down the crease of his round, taut ass. "I'm gonna miss this ass now you're retired."

He turns and tilts his head. "Meaning?"

My cock pushes inside, and I let out a slow, long breath,

letting my throbbing dick calm down. "Now you're not on a strict workout schedule, this tight bubble butt is gonna get all saggy and soft. So is this." I reach around and run my hand down his chiseled chest and abs. "You're gonna be my big, soft marshmallow."

"Kinda losing my erection here."

"Nah. I can't wait for it." I lean over him again and pepper soft kisses along his shoulder and up to his neck while moving in and out of him at a languid pace. Next to his ear, I whisper, "Because I'm gonna love you in every shape, every age, any which way you are for the rest of our lives."

"Marc …"

My name on Miller's lips in the whiny and needy way he says it … I pull back and slam inside him.

He calls out, and I do it again.

Miller starts pushing backward, trying to get me to go faster. His body is begging for it while he lets out agonized moan after moan.

"I promise," I say, panting, running out of breath now.

We may be already covered in grease, but now we're covered in sweat too.

"I promise my life to you. I know we're about to go out there and say this in front of everyone we know, but I wanted to tell you here and now. Just us."

"I love you, Marc." Miller's big and powerful body trembles in my hands.

I move to grip his cock. "Show me. Come for me."

He lets go, his body tightening and giving in at the same time.

I continue to fill him with my cock until my legs go weak and I come inside him. "Love you," I breathe.

"Clean up," Miller grunts.

With a small laugh, I pull out of him and reach for a hand towel on a hook on the wall and run it under warm water.

Miller looks wrung out and thoroughly fucked.

My work here is done. I can't hide my smugness no matter how hard I try.

"Shut up," he grumbles.

We're both wobbly on our legs, but I try to help wipe him down as well as I can with what little towel I have.

We barely get a chance to get clean when there's a loud bang on the bathroom door.

"Hurry up," Vanessa calls.

"Told you we didn't have time," Miller says.

"Hey, we technically had enough time. We just didn't have enough time for both sex *and* to clean up."

We try to rush through it, but grease is a bitch to wash off. Who knew?

There's another bang on the door. "Tuxes are here, and people are waaaaaiting. If I wasn't scared about what I'd walk in on, I'd come in there and get you myself."

Yep. Vanessa can be scary.

"I'll go get your agent," she threatens.

Really scary.

"Fuck, good enough." Miller uses a second towel to try to dry himself, but it doesn't really work when the towel is small and he's so … Miller. "We're gonna have to drip-dry." He slips his underwear back on.

I'm still trying to get grease off me. "This shit is everywhere."

Miller laughs. "City boy."

I give him the finger. "First thing to do when we get back to the hotel is shower."

"Uh-huh. Right after I have a go at your ass. Flipping is only fair."

Even though we just finished having sex, my cock twitches and my ass clenches, already anticipating tonight. "How long is the ceremony again?"

"Don't forget the reception too." Miller approaches. "Your ass is going to have to wait at least the next eight hours."

"Whose idea was this wedding?" I grumble.

"*Yours.*"

"Fuck, I hate me."

There's a knock on the door again, but this time it opens.

Damon steps through and folds his arms. "Are you getting married sometime today or what?"

"Yeah, yeah, we're coming."

Damon eyes my naked form. "Like that? Didn't realize it was that type of wedding. At least you'll give the paparazzi something to photograph."

Our heads swivel as if disconnected from our bodies.

"Paparazzi?" Miller asks.

"Uh, yeah. That was my way of breaking it to you. When the hired security guys wouldn't let them through the gates to the venue, a couple of them climbed a fence. The town cop is handling it, but don't be surprised if any more pop out at you on your way to the aisle."

Great. Just great. So much for the privacy of doing this wedding out of town.

"Think of it this way? Free wedding photographers?"

We both glare at him.

"Okay, I'm, uh, gonna go make sure no more paparazzi get in."

"You do that." I sigh.

Miller wraps his arms around me. "It's okay."

"It's *annoying*."

"It's the third thing out of the way."

Huh? "Third thing?"

"You know how they say bad things come in threes? We had the car break down, forgot the tuxes, and now paparazzi. That's it. All hiccups done now." He kisses me softly. "So, let's get dressed and get out there."

"Last ten minutes as a single guy. You sure you're ready?" I ask.

"Oh, I'm ready."

Me too. More than ready.

CHAPTER TWENTY-ONE

MILLER

Talon walks down the pebbled aisle first with both his parents by his side, and my mom and I follow. Neither one of us wanted to be the one "waiting" at the end of the aisle. Talon and I started this thing together and we'll walk out of here together, because that's what this wedding is about.

Talon and me. Forever.

I've always been enamored by Marcus Talon, and until he kissed me in a hospital bathroom while I was on so many meds I couldn't even be sure he was actually kissing me, I didn't believe in soul mates.

Now? As I take my spot at the altar, I have no doubt that the man standing next to me was created to be mine.

A breeze passes through the lush gardens, but it isn't enough to stop me from sweating in this monkey suit.

Talon looks as handsome as ever, like he always does in a tux. But, hell, my man looks good in anything.

His blue eyes shine but not in the mischievous way they

usually do. They're glassy with emotion I don't think I can handle without bawling like a baby.

But as his steady hands take my shaky ones and hold firm, he grounds me and keeps me focused.

The officiant does his thing, talking about love between two souls, how love doesn't discriminate, and how the beauty that is all-round encompassing love doesn't see gender.

It perfectly describes Talon and me.

Our lives have been intertwined in some form since I was eighteen years old. Now, twelve years later, we're sealing it with a promise.

When it's time to say my vows, I take in a deep breath.

"I know marriage isn't going to be easy. It's not going to be a touchdown on a breakaway or a completed pass to the end zone."

There are a few snickers at the football analogies, but what do they expect? I may be retired, but I'm a football player in my heart.

"But being married to you will be the easiest thing I've ever done, because all I've wanted since I met you was to be with you. Next to you. I want nothing more than for you to be happy, and I'm honored, humbled, and eager to call myself your husband."

Talon's lips quirk the tiniest bit, and when it's his turn, he's the calm and collected Talon he is on the field. Always cool under pressure.

"I don't have many regrets in life. I'm not the type of person to hold on to the past. But if I could go back and change anything, I'd change being so blinded, young, and dumb when it came to you. You were my best friend throughout college, and I should have known that empty feeling in my heart when

I graduated was because of you. We might have lost our way for a while there, but we found each other again, and I don't ever want to be apart."

I will not cry. I will not cry.

I'm a big, masculine, offensive tackle.

We don't do tears.

Talon continues. "In the words of a great philosopher, 'If you live to be a hundred, I want to live to be a hundred minus one day, so I never have to live without you.'"

Aww fuck, I'm crying.

He leans in and whispers, "That great philosopher is Winnie the Pooh, by the way."

I burst out laughing. Fucking Talon.

His vows are him in a nutshell.

We exchange rings, I manage to hold my shit together for the rest of the ceremony, and after we're officially married, we seal it with a kiss that's tame compared to how we usually go at it.

Lucky too, because at that precise moment, a photographer, who's not the one we hired, appears out of nowhere and snaps the money shot.

That guy's bills have been paid for the next year.

He takes off running immediately after, and Officer Silas and a guy who I think is our florist run after him. We'll let them deal with it, because nothing can tear us down right now.

Walking back down the aisle with my brand-new husband, I don't let go of his hand for even a second while everyone stops us to congratulate and hug us.

And at the very end, there stands eight guys who are just as much family as our blood relatives.

Our agent, Damon. His non-husband, Maddox. Our brother

on the field, Matt. Sarcastic Noah. My future work colleague, Lennon. The hockey players, Ollie and Soren, and the baby brother of the group, Jet.

They all wear matching smiles.

They're all so important to us.

Since our Fiji vacation, we've all been spread around the country. We don't get to see each other often as individual couples, let alone get to be in the same room together as an entire group.

Talon holds out his arms. "Group hug?"

"Group hug," we all say.

Then we're all arms as we form a huddle, and I can only hope that the hand on my ass belongs to my husband.

A little whine interrupts our lovefest.

"Aww, is that my honorary niece?" Talon coos and pulls away.

Matt and Noah's daughter, Jackie, squirms in her stroller.

"Hi, baby girl." Talon picks her up. "Did you get jealous of all the hugging because no one was paying attention to you?"

Damn.

I have no idea why that's so hot, but it is. It warms my heart.

I can't wait for Talon to be a dad and for us to do it together.

The baby breaks into a wide smile at her uncle Talon, and Matt and Noah both melt behind him.

They're so in love with her.

Talon turns to me. "I may be rethinking our timeline."

My face lights up. "Really?"

He nods. "I want kids now."

I step forward. "Let's just take this one."

Matt laughs. "Nice try." He takes the baby off Talon.

I shrug. "Worth a shot."

Noah looks around the group. "So if Talon and Miller are having kids, which of you guys are next?"

All six of them put their fingers to their nose and say, "Not it."

Noah snickers.

The official wedding photographer squeezes her way into the group. "We're going to need to start getting photos before we lose the light."

Talon smiles. "You can start right here with these guys. They're our family."

We didn't do the whole wedding party thing, but if we had, there's no doubt this group of guys would be it.

She moves us away from the ceremony area to a wall of flowers and gets us to line up.

It's like herding cats, honestly.

But in the hustle of trying to organize us, the photographer takes candids. I already know the photo that will be framed on our mantel won't be the last shot—the one where we're all standing straight and smiling at the camera.

It'll be the one where Talon has me in a headlock. The one where Matt and Noah are fussing over their baby girl. Where Maddox and Damon are kissing, Lennon's looking up at Ollie lovingly, and Jet's sticking his tongue out at Soren while flipping off the camera.

Because that's the photo that's *us*.

V
_____

JET AND SOREN

CHAPTER TWENTY-TWO

JET

"Ah, we're back in Fiji," Soren says and holds his arms out.

The sand between my toes feels wrong, the breeze is weird, and this in no way feels like Fiji. Fiji is the place I fell in love for real the very first time. Not confusing love, not comforting love, but true love. The kind of shit Disney movies are made of.

"Fake Fiji," I complain. "It's not the same."

Soren wraps his arm around me. "Hey, it's the closest we're gonna get anytime soon."

The soundstage decked out to make it look like a beach with industrial-sized fans to create fake wind is nowhere near the same feeling of real Fiji.

With Soren's team making it to the playoffs and then my band's tour kicking off pretty much the minute the Stanley Cup was won—not by New Jersey, *sorry, babe*—we've barely had time to breathe let alone take another vacation.

Hell, we barely have time to go to Chicago to wish my

niece a happy first birthday. We're flying out of L.A. tomorrow to spend a few days with family before starting the European leg of Radioactive's tour.

"You two ready?" the director asks.

Am I ready? Not really. This was a stupid idea to begin with. "As ready as we'll ever be to splash our love story everywhere for the entire world to see."

"There's the spirit!"

Clearly, the director needs me to hold up a sarcasm sign when I speak.

When Harley, my ex and cowriter of this song, suggested this for the music video, I thought the label wouldn't go for it. The song itself basically screams sexual-identity crisis. It's called "Confusion" for fuck's sake. Putting a same-sex couple in the video will only cement it.

There wouldn't be a problem with that if this song was mine and mine alone, but it's not.

Harley Valentine's brand is attached to it, and he has spent so many years hiding his sexuality from the public.

And while he's still technically engaged to a woman, I wonder how long that façade will last after this song comes out.

It honestly wouldn't shock me if the label buries the song and never releases the video. I'm surprised it's gotten this far. When they dropped it from his first solo album since splitting with the boy band, Eleven, I thought it wouldn't see the light of day, but here we are, about to drop it into the world in a surprise release.

Soren and I get on a jet ski in front of a green screen.

One of my stipulations for this video was that Soren feature in it with me. I didn't want some random model, especially when the storyboard is about us falling in love while Harley's "character" watches from the sidelines.

It's not exactly how it happened in real life but close enough. Also, awkward as fuck, but that's a whole other issue.

I'd originally said no to the whole idea, because I didn't want to be involved in their publicity games, but when I mentioned it to Soren, he jumped at the chance. Said it'd be something cool to show the grandkids.

Of course, that tripped me up, because to have grandkids, we'd need to have actual kids.

He said, "In the future. Duh."

He hasn't brought it up since.

I don't know if I should be allowed to look after someone else. I can barely look after myself. I'm allergic to responsibility.

A few months ago at Talon and Miller's wedding, Soren was one of the first to say no to kids.

Now suddenly we have hypothetical grandchildren.

But I haven't said anything. It's for future me to deal with.

Soren's arms trail down my naked torso. "Hey, what does this remind you of?"

"Stop fucking touching me. I can't have a hard-on for this video."

But it's too late. I can't help thinking of our time in Fiji. The wind in my hair as we sped across the water. Soren's hand in my shorts, stroking my dick until I came everywhere.

"God, I hate you," I mutter and try to think of unsexy things.

Like my brothers. Umm, chicken. My brothers eating chicken.

Okay, that works.

The director steps up to us. "All right, guys. We'll run playback, but I don't want you lip-syncing this shot."

"What will we be doing, then?" I ask.

"I want you looking back at your partner, and, Soren, you need to lean forward a bit to catch the right light. It'll feel awkward, but it's best for the camera. You're to look like you're about to kiss without actually kissing."

Soren smiles. "I dunno if it'll be possible not to kiss him when he's that close, but I'll try."

The director huffs impatiently and stalks back behind his camera.

I elbow him. "We need to be *professional*."

"Hey, you're the musician here. I'm just an extra in this video."

"If you distract me, we're gonna be here all night, so please behave?"

Soren's lips purse. "Isn't that usually my line? Oh, how the tables have turned. Is this what it's like to be you? I could get used to it." He playfully runs his hand down my side.

I shiver from his touch, recoil when he hits somewhere I'm ticklish, and get frustrated that we can't get out of here and do this elsewhere.

"Well, don't get used to it, because you know I can only hold my maturity together for short periods of time, and I really, really, really wanna go home so we can fuck."

Soren wiggles behind me as if to get comfortable and clears his throat. "Best behavior. Promise."

Knew that would pull him back in line.

"We're rolling," the director says.

The playback begins, and Harley's voice fills the room. I

try to contain my wince, but our whole situation makes me cringe.

Soren, the only man in this world for me, cups my face and whispers, "Hey. It's just you and me."

He knows me like no one else. He knows I'm not comfortable even though this is my job and I fucking *rock* at it—pun intended. Signing on to do a duet with Harley was a great move for my career, but I'd be lying if I said it doesn't suck tying my career to Harley's for the foreseeable future.

We'll have to talk about each other, do talk shows and other media commitments together, and make surprise guest appearances at one another's concerts.

It's not that I hate the guy or even still have feelings for him, but I want that part of my life closed off from what I have now, which is happiness I never knew could happen to me.

Watching my brother Matt fall in love with Noah, I knew that type of forever existed in the world, but after three years in the music biz and being treated like a rent boy by fans and management alike, I figured it would never happen for *me*. Not while I was living this life.

Then Soren comes barreling back into existence after years of trying to pretend we didn't mean anything to each other.

Staring into the warm, honey-colored eyes of my boyfriend, I can't imagine being without him ever again.

And now he's finished out his last season and is retired, I don't have to.

We keep staring at each other for the cameras, barely moving and slowly tilting our heads as if we're going to kiss.

Soren's lips part slightly, and he's right. This is going to be hard to have him right there without being allowed to close the small gap and touch my mouth to his.

I knew from our first kiss that Soren would change my life. I just didn't know how.

He makes my breathing shallow, my heartbeat erratic, and his touch makes my soul want to spout sonnets about belonging to him.

What we have is intense.

The way he cares for me, claims me, the way he's piercing me with his gaze right now … his love is palpable.

Soren blurts something that sounds like "Merry men."

At the same time, the director says, "And cut."

I cock my head at Soren. "Merry men? Like, Robin Hood's fuck buddies?" What's that got to do with anything?

Soren's eyes widen, and he turns his attention to the director. "We good?"

"Yup, got the shot. Let's move on. This time, Jay, I need you lip-syncing and looking at the camera while acting like you're speeding across the water. Soren, just be natural. Kiss his neck, shoulder, whatever."

"Hear that?" I smirk at Soren. "You get to kiss my whatever."

He doesn't reply. His face pulls a weird expression I can't decipher. Kinda like he's freaking out?

"Not what I meant," the director cuts in. "This isn't that type of shoot."

I snicker.

We run it again. And then again.

It's the only thing I hate about music video shoots—long days doing the same thing over and over again for hours of footage that'll be edited into three minutes of awesome.

Soren shifts from his playful self to his professional and serious self, but it's not a gradual thing. It's like a switch flip. I think he's over it already, and we're only about halfway through the day.

We change scenes and change wardrobe countless times, and his mood doesn't seem to improve.

He doesn't seem angry, just … flat.

Finally, we end with a scene at a night club on a dance floor where we're finally allowed to kiss.

The storyboard had Harley watching us with longing in his eyes, but because we don't have to interact, we agreed to film on separate days.

It's easier that way.

I doubt this scene will make the final cut. While a few videos might have brief LGBTQ representation, this is still open to censorship.

When we're finally directed to kiss, it's damn explosive. We've spent the last few hours being unable to close that small distance between us. Now we're allowed, there's no holding back the eruption of passion in every second that passes with our mouths pressed together.

This is where I belong.

The director calls cut, and Soren tries to pull away, but I don't let him. I don't care we're in a room full of producers, extras, and crew for the video. I'm not ready for it to end.

That is, until the director says the words I've been wanting to hear all day. "That's a wrap."

I pull back. "Let's go home."

Soren smiles wide—a smile that always turns my insides upside down.

He takes my hand, and we move to walk off set and toward wardrobe to exchange our video outfits for our civilian clothes, but my feet pause at the sight of someone I shouldn't be seeing.

We agreed he wasn't going to be here.

Harley folds his arms and sticks out his chin.

In a move to keep civility, I approach my ex-boyfriend. We have to work together for the foreseeable future. We've agreed to play nice, but we also agreed he wouldn't be here for my filming, so ...

"I thought you weren't on the schedule today?" I say, directing blame on someone else fucking up instead of accusing him of breaking our deal.

Harley hangs his head. "I wasn't. They called me in for reshoots. Said you'd be done by now."

"Oh. Uh, yeah, we ran a little overtime." Or a lot.

"I can see why. You two look great together."

"I didn't know you were here—"

"It's okay," Harley says. "These things always take longer than they expect."

"I mean, I wouldn't have, uh, been so ..."

"Enthusiastic?" Harley finishes for me.

"Uh, yeah, that. If I knew you were here, I would've—"

"It's been a year. I'm over it." He shrugs but doesn't give me eye contact, and I know him too well not to see that he's hiding his pain behind his casual demeanor.

When we recorded the song together, I admitted to him that I never loved him the way I thought I did. It took getting together with Soren to realize what Harley and I had, while real, was still very much a relationship of convenience.

He didn't agree with that assessment, and we've barely spoken since. When we have, it's only been about the song.

We fall silent, and yep, this is exactly what I expected

would happen when we'd see each other again. We've both been busy, and with the label cutting this song from the album, I thought we wouldn't have to deal with being in the same place at the same time unless it was for some music awards or whatever.

Harley's gaze goes to Soren. "Good to see you again, hockey player."

As polite as that is, it's also totally fake. Soren replies with a "You too" which is just as fake as Harley's.

"We need to get out of here," I say. "Good luck with your shoot."

The director steps in. "Oh, you're all good to go home. We got the shot during the last take."

Harley cocks his head. "You did?"

"Plenty of emotion as you watched these two on the dance floor."

Just how long was Harley standing here?

Harley looks horrified. "You were filming me … that … the …"

"Relax. It was great. Trust me."

Mine and Soren's gazes ping-pong between the director and Harley.

"We'll, uh, leave you to deal with this," I say, and Soren and I head for wardrobe to the sounds of Harley protesting the background and lighting isn't right and they need to reshoot.

I feel a little guilty for the way things ended between us, because essentially it was neither of our faults.

The label just puts so much pressure on him, and I don't know why or how he puts up with it.

I wish for him to find someone so he can be as happy as I am with Soren.

Someone who isn't famous.

Someone who takes him for who he is and appreciates his work ethic and drive.

Someone who supports him.

He deserves happiness even if the industry we're in is adamant in making him choose between career and love.

He needs to find that person who makes him question the worthiness of his music compared to what he could have if he let go.

"Well, that was fun," Soren says sarcastically.

"I get the feeling all of our future dealings with him will be like that."

"Can't wait."

Even though he mocks it, I know he holds no ill feelings toward Harley. He doesn't need to, because he knows I'm his.

I'll be his forever if that's what he wants.

All he has to do is ask.

CHAPTER TWENTY-THREE

SOREN

I can't believe I blurted a marriage proposal during a video shoot. What I can't believe even more is that the director yelled cut right at that same moment. I'm both thankful and regretful for the interruption. While I'm happy Jet didn't hear me properly and I get a chance at a do-over, part of me wishes he had known what I said. At least then I wouldn't have this itching need to put it out there again.

I hadn't planned on asking him. We've only been together a year, and we haven't even discussed it. But like any time Jet's that close to me, he consumes my every thought and I get lost in the moment. It's easy to lose focus when Jet's around.

And today, all I wanted to do was show him how much I belong with him.

I want him to stare at a ring on his finger and know he's loved, know he's not alone, and know he's mine.

But this is something that needs to be done right. I shouldn't blurt it out in a room full of strangers and his ex-boyfriend. It should be perfect.

No pressure, Soren.

When we get back to the mansion we're currently sharing with Benji and Freya—Jet's bandmates—we make our way to our bedroom.

Jet's hands are wandering, and his lips move all over my neck and chest.

I want to let go and enjoy it, but I have shit to plan, damn it. And I need to do it now before I go blurting it out again at the wrong moment.

"Baby?"

Jet pulls back. "What's wrong?"

"I just remembered Freya wanted to talk to me about something when we got home."

He frowns. "What?"

"I don't know. Benji maybe? You know them. Drama, drama, drama."

"Ugh. Tell me about it. It's only gotten worse since they ran off to a chapel in Vegas and tied the knot. Now they're stuck with each other for life. Or until they get divorced. One or the other."

I pause, and my heart thunders. "I-is that what you think of marriage?"

"Doomed to be stuck together forever or end in a bitter argument? Pretty much." Jet purses his lips. "Actually, no. I take that back. I've seen how good it can be. Like with Matt and Noah. Marriage as a whole is kinda an outdated construct. It started because of ownership, for fuck's sake. And not in the way you say you own me. More like in the 'You get no choice' way. So thinking about it in those terms, it makes me ask, 'Why bother,' but then I see Matt and Noah and think, 'Yeah, they're doing it right.'" He glances at me. "Sorry, I'm rambling."

I pull him close and kiss the tip of his nose. "I love your rambling." Especially because I want to promise him the type of marriage he believes in. "I'll be back soon, okay?"

"Can't you talk to her in the morning? It's late, and I need your cock."

I groan. There is no way I can get through fucking him without proposing. "You can have it. Right after I talk to Freya. Why don't you go and get ready for me?"

Jet smirks. "Hurry up. Tell her to forgive Benji for whatever he's done now and come to bed."

My vision more includes telling Benji and Freya not to come downstairs so he can tackle me as soon as I propose and ride me right there on the back deck. We can't let all the prepping he's about to do go to waste.

Jet heads inside our room while I make my way to the other end of the house where Benji and Freya live.

I knock on Benji's door, because they mostly sleep in there. Seeing as Freya didn't actually ask me to talk to her, I assume she's with him and they're not actually fighting. "Freya?"

No response.

I try again but louder.

Movement inside the room sounds, and then a half-asleep Freya appears, her hair wild, one eye open.

She grunts.

"Do you, umm, I don't know, have like candles and shit?"

She cocks her head. "Candles?"

"I'm trying to make a big grand gesture, and candlelight is, like, romantic? Or something?"

Now she's glaring. "And you think waking me up to be romantic is important, because ..."

I lower my voice even though Jet wouldn't be able to hear anyway. "Because this is the biggest grand gesture I'll ever make in my entire life?"

Hint, hint.

Her eyes widen. "Oh my God, this is so awesome." She throws her arms around me. "Welcome to the family. Like properly. Even though you're already one of us. But this is like ... official!"

"Thanks, but shh, he has no idea. So, umm, candles?"

"I'm happy for you guys, truly, but what makes you think I have all that stuff?"

"You're a girl."

"Pfft. She ain't that type of girl." Benji appears, handing me four giant candles. "Here."

I can't help laughing.

"I'll leave you two to go back to sleep." I hold up the candles. "Thanks for this."

"Wait, I have more." He pulls out a plastic bag from his closet, but instead of giving it to me, he follows me downstairs.

Watching this big, burly Aussie guy place tealight candles delicately around the deck is adorable.

He senses me watching him. "Chicks dig romance."

I chuckle. "Thanks for helping."

"Anytime. This is a massive step."

I nod. "It is, but I'm ready for it. I don't ever want to live without him."

Benji smiles wide. "I'm happy it only took you a few years to pull your head out of your ass, mate."

Yeah, yeah. I did the stupidest thing four years ago when I thought Jet needed to go and be young and live his life.

It's not the first time that I've wondered what would have been had we tried to make it work back then, but Jet was only twenty. The experiences he's had since then make him the man he is today, and I wouldn't ever want to take that away from him.

I'd take back the hurt I caused him and the anguish that made him write two multi-platinum songs. But then he wouldn't be as famous as he is.

We almost get all the candles lit when Benji tells me to go get Jet and he'll light the last few, then make himself scarce.

"Thanks, Benji."

"Anything for Jet."

It's weird when his bandmates call him by his real name and not his stage name Jay. They've gotten used to the name change over the years, and so he's always Jay to them. But Benji using Jet's name now means he understands how monumental this moment is.

Then Benji gets a weird glimmer in his eyes. "I know you all think Freya and I are nothing but drama, but there's no doubt in my mind she's it for me. When you know, you know."

I nod. It's true. We often wonder how they will work when they constantly fight, but it's how they've always been and how they probably always will be. They're not abusive toward each other or anything. They just love getting riled up and yelling at each other followed by angry sex.

It works for them.

"When you know, you know," I repeat.

I know Jet is the one for me.

There's no room in my heart for anyone else when he owns it wholly and completely.

Unfortunately, something else has my man's heart, and as I make my way back upstairs to get him, I realize my fatal mistake.

Sleep. Jet needs sleep.

We've been on tour for months. We just had a full day filming, and he ran into Harley which always leaves him drained. Tomorrow we fly to Chicago to celebrate Jackie's birthday, and then two days later we're off to see my parents in Toronto before flying to London to start the European leg of his tour.

He's exhausted, and he only managed to pull his pants underneath his ass so his cute butt is sticking out.

There's lube on the bed, the cap off, but I doubt he used it before falling asleep.

I sigh and head back down to Benji.

He's hunched over, lighting some tealight candles on the floor. "Wait, wait," he says. "It's not ready!"

I wait for him to finish, and when he moves away, I see he has spelled out "I love you" in tealights.

"Aww, I love you too, but you can blow it out," I say.

He turns to me. "What's wrong?"

"Poor guy is passed out."

"Then wake him up!"

I laugh. "I'm not going to propose to a pissed-off Jet. You know what he's like if he's woken up."

"Oh. True."

Before we can extinguish any of the flames, we flinch at the croaky voice behind us. "Propose?"

I turn to find Jet standing in the doorway, his pants

securely back on but a confused look on his face.

No, this wasn't how it was supposed to go!

"I ... uh ..."

"I'm out." Benji makes a run for it, but as he passes Jet, he pats him on the back.

"Propose?" Jet asks again.

He glances around the back deck, at all the candles, and then his gaze lands on the *I love you.*

"I fell asleep." He sounds like he's still not awake entirely.

I chuckle. "Yeah, you did. I was about to pack all of this up."

"I heard you come in, but then you left, and ..." His deep brown eyes meet mine. "Am I dreaming? Am I still upstairs in bed?"

Fuck, he's so cute.

I approach him and drag him toward the candles.

He keeps glancing between me and the ground.

I lift his chin with my finger to get him to focus on me. When he does, nerves kick me in the stomach.

Deep breath, Soren. "Jet, I love you more than anything else in this world. It's the type of love I never knew existed. And today, while we were filming together and working as a team, I realized I will never want anyone else. Ever ... For the rest of my life."

Jet looks confused for a second before he gasps. "Merry men. You didn't say merry men."

I shake my head. "I didn't. It was the wrong place to do it, and maybe this isn't the most perfect place either—I don't even have a ring—but I can't have another day pass where you don't know what you are to me. You're everything I've ever wanted, and I'm going to give you the type of marriage you believe in. I'll be a husband who supports you, cares for you, and be there for you through everything."

Jet sniffs, and in the flickering light, I see a small tear drop from his eye.

I wipe it with my thumb. "I won't let outside influences distract from my feelings for you or take me away from what's important. I will always put *us* first because it's you and me. Always."

"I knew you were it," Jet whispers. "The one. The night I met you, I knew you'd change my life. You ended up showing me what love could be even if you couldn't give it back then."

"I want to give it to you now. All of it." I lower myself to my knee and take hold of his hand. "Jethro Jackson, will you marry me?"

Jet's lip trembles as he nods. "Yes." He sniffs again. "Fuck, I can't even make a joke about there being no ring, because I love this more. It's … perfect."

I get off my knee. "I promise to give you everything you want. Everything you *need*."

"And I promise to take it." Jet smirks. "But for real. I want to give you everything too. Something you said about the video shoot made me freak out a little, I'm not gonna lie—"

"The grandkids comment? Because that means we actually have to have children?"

He nods.

"I figured as much. We don't have to do that if you don't want to."

"I want to," he gurgles as if he has trouble getting the words out. "I mean, I need to win some Grammys first. Live this insane lifestyle for a while before we settle down, but I want to. Maybe when I'm forty."

"Baby, I think you need to do some math. If we wait until you're forty, I'll be fifty. I won't even live to see grandkids then."

"Oh right. You're like old. I forget that. How about when I'm thirty."

"I can handle thirty."

A glimmer shines in my fiancé's eyes.

Wow. *Fiancé.*

"Did we really just get engaged?" I ask.

Jet chuckles. "Unless I wake up and this *is* all a dream."

I pull him close. "Not a dream."

"Prove it," he taunts.

I'm about to kiss him for the millionth time, but I've never anticipated Jet's lips more. I want to put everything I have into it and kiss him so hard he'll never be able to doubt me, us, or the future we're promising each other.

Our breaths mingle.

Only a centimeter away, Jet says, "Caleb?"

I both love and hate when he uses my first name. Love it in moments like this, but it's rare for him to use it adoringly.

"I love you so damn much," he whispers.

He doesn't allow me to say it back because he crushes his mouth to mine.

It's explosive, it's loving, and it's so fucking hot.

My cock grows hard. The need I always have for him simmering under the surface boils over, and I wish I could take him right here and now. I want to claim him with my body while promising him forever with my words.

I groan. "I don't suppose you got the chance to do as I asked before falling asleep upstairs?"

Jet breathes heavy. "Why don't you find out for yourself?"

My hand trails down his back and dips into his jeans. His hole is slick and waiting for me. My fingers tease him.

The shudder that runs through him triggers my own need.

Jet suddenly grips my T-shirt tight and pulls me toward the padded deck chairs. He pushes me down so I lie on the reclined chair. "I don't have the energy for teasing. Undo your pants."

I love bossy Jet.

While I fumble with my belt and fly, Jet lifts his shirt over his head and drops his jeans and boxer briefs to the ground.

The houses in this area are pretty close together, but neither one of us cares right now about giving our neighbors a show. Not with how desperate we are.

Jet climbs into my lap completely naked and sinks down on my exposed cock. My shirt is still on, my pants are down to my thighs, and as much as I'd love to even the playing field right now and lose my clothes, Jet's tight and not completely prepped hole is too busy causing little shocks of pleasure to shoot through me.

His mouth comes back down on mine, and he moans as his body takes more of me.

I want to take this slow and do it properly—love him tenderly—but there's no holding back.

We've gone past the vows of cherish and moved onto worship. I would pray in the name of Jet's ass if he asked me to. That doesn't even make sense, but with every rotation of his hips, every single inch of me that moves inside him, my brain loses sense. It only knows one thing, and that's how to love Jet the way Jet deserves.

I plant my feet either side of the deck chair and sit up.

Jet's ass clamps around my cock, but he doesn't stop

moving.

Our bodies meet over and over and over at a slower pace now because Jet's in my lap, this chair is flimsy, and our position doesn't give us the most room to move.

So I stand with Jet still in my arms, his legs wrapped around me, and I drop my pants so I don't trip on them.

I move us indoors and over to the large sectional couch.

My dick slips out of him, and he whimpers.

"Just a sec, baby." I drop him onto the plush material, grab his knees and push them up, and dive back in.

He cries out as I must hit his prostate, and I don't even bother to tell him to be quiet.

Benji and Freya would know exactly what we're doing. There's no way they'll come down again tonight.

Now in this better position, I can fuck him as hard as I want.

I cover his body with mine and rest my head on his shoulder while I pump into him.

His hands claw at my back under my shirt, sure to leave scratch marks, but it doesn't slow me down.

My arms are slick with sweat, and so is my hair.

I rest up on my elbows and stare down at Jet, who looks like a perfect glowing angel with his pale skin and cherublike curly hair hanging loosely around his face.

He's always gorgeous, there's no doubt about that, but right now he has this primal and feral look in his eye as I take his body. I may be the one claiming him, but I'm already his.

The second I reach between us and touch his cock, he explodes. His eyes close and his mouth drops open. The sight of him coming always pushes me over the edge.

I come inside him and collapse on top of his smaller frame.

I'd try to avoid putting all my weight on him, but my muscles are jelly.

"Babe?" Jet rasps.

"Yeah?" I'm just as breathless.

"We're getting married."

I smile. "Hell yeah, we are."

I drop lazy kisses all over my fiancé's chest to wake him up the next day.

"No," he grumbles.

I should feel guilty about keeping him up last night when he really does need rest, but I'm a selfish guy who will never feel guilty about loving my man and showing him how much.

"We're going to be late to the airport," I say.

Jet grumbles some more. "I swear Jackie is lucky she's so damn adorable."

He gets out of bed, but the complaining doesn't stop until we get to the airport and get some coffee into him.

He gets some more sleep on the plane, and by the time we land in Chicago and we're chauffeured to our hotel room, we have exactly one hour before we need to leave for Matt and Noah's place.

They offered for us to crash there, but they've got a full house now with a baby and Wade. Plus, I'd be worried one would try to stab me in my sleep.

Especially after we tell them we're engaged. That's going to be fun.

I don't think they'll ever get over their protectiveness of their little brother.

Poor Jackie is going to have it ten times worse.

I unpack some nicer button-down shirts and hang them in the hotel room's closet.

Jet's rummaging through his bag when he stops suddenly and looks up at me. He either just got the best idea ever, or I've done something wrong. I'm not sure which yet because his face is more shock than any other emotion.

"We should get married while we're here," he blurts.

I glance around the small suite. "Umm, it's kinda impersonal. And I'm pretty sure we need rings and an official person to, like, marry us and stuff."

"You're sooo funny. I mean while we're in *Chicago*. Everyone's here for Jackie's birthday, and I don't want a circus like Talon and Miller's wedding. Just bing, bang, boom, done. Get it over with."

"Aww, you're sooo romantic." Though I'm definitely not opposed to the idea. The sooner I get to call Jet my husband, the better. Hell, I really would marry him in this room right now if we could.

"It's not the wedding I want. It's the marriage." Jet's words are soft and a little unsure.

Jet being unsure in anything he says is his vulnerability slipping through.

I smile. "Let's do it. I'll need to fly my family out, and what about your people? Benji, Freya, Marty, Luce—"

Jet shakes his head. "Benji and Freya are doing a few talk show appearances for the band before the Europe tour kicks off, and Luce will be with them. But maybe we can try to live stream it for them."

"That's easy. Is there a waiting period or anything for marriage licensing? There's so much to do, and—"

"There's a lot to do." Jet's hand runs up my arm and lands on my chest. "But we'll do it together." After a soft kiss to my lips, he steps back. "I'll get the marriage license info, you call your parents."

It's surprisingly easy to book a courthouse wedding. We just have to stop by the county clerk's office to pick up the license today for a tomorrow wedding. It takes longer to book my family's flights.

It makes us late to get to Jackie's birthday party, but I'm sure we'll be forgiven when we explain.

Shit. We have to actually explain.

"I have a brilliant idea," I say to Jet when we're in the car on the way.

"Is it as brilliant as my idea to get married tomorrow?"

"Even brillianter."

"That's not a word."

I shrug. "Are you ready for it?"

"I don't know, am I?"

"What if …" I start. "I just meet you tomorrow at the courthouse and you can tell all your brothers?" I'm joking. Mostly.

Jet laughs. "Are you seriously scared of them?"

I scoff. "Not at all," I lie. "After a few death threats, they'll be fine." I hope. "And you know we're somehow going to end up in a strip club by the end of the night."

"Truth."

"All right. Private room is booked at City Boys for tonight to celebrate," Talon says.

I laugh and cock my eyebrow at Jet. "Told you."

"Hello. We have a baby." Noah points to Jackie. "Not taking her to a strip club."

"Isn't that why you hired a nanny?" Talon asks.

Matt laughs. "Ooh, I cannot wait until your son is born in a few months. Let's see how many times you're willing to leave him with a nanny."

"Are you saying you're not going to your own brother's bachelor party?"

Talon's going to make a great parent, because his guilting skills are on point.

"No, we'll go," Matt grumbles. "But just you wait." Matt takes Jackie into his arms and cuddles her close.

I can't wait for that to happen for us, but the reasons why Jet wants to wait are valid. His touring schedule for the next few years is going to be insane, and I want to be with him. The road is no place for a kid.

We have dinner at Matt and Noah's and wait for Jackie to go to sleep and the nanny to show up before we head out.

I get by with only a few threats from the guys, warning me against hurting Jet. Words like shotguns and body bags are thrown around.

But if there's one thing I'm sure of, it's that I'm marrying the man of my dreams, and the last thing I ever want to do is hurt him.

It doesn't take long for Jet to get into the night. And by that, I mean, he is served countless drinks from the minute we step into the club.

That's how we end up here hours later—where I can't take my eyes off him as he spins around the pole in the group's private room while the actual stripper watches on in amusement.

Matt stepped out to call and check on the baby, but Noah's in the corner covering his eyes.

Ollie leans over to me. "Your future husband is drunk."

He sure as fuck is.

The fluorescent lights make Jet's smile brighter. His eyes are glassy, his face flushed, and he just radiates happy.

I did that. Not the alcohol. *Me.*

There isn't a moment that goes by where I wonder *what if* anymore.

None of it matters now when, tomorrow, my lonely, Southern, sweet, and sarcastic rock star is going to be officially mine forever.

A song kicks in through the speakers of the room, one I don't recognize, but Jet lets out a "Whoop. I love this song. Babe. Babe. Hey, babe. Get up here."

I shake my head. "I'm good. Dance with the stripper."

Jet scowls. "Caleb Sorensen. If I wanted to dance with a stripper, I'd be marrying him tomorrow, not you. Get your ass up here now."

"Uh-oh, you're in trouble," Ollie says next to me.

Jet pulls me up next to the stripper, whose eyes are as wide as his insane pecs.

"Y-you guys are getting married?"

"In secret. Please don't tip off any paparazzi," I beg.

"He can't!" Jet slurs. "I'm pretty sure there's stripper-customer confidentiality. Like lawyers but with less clothes!"

"That is true," the stripper says. "But only if a big tip is involved." Then he has the balls to wink.

I reach into my back pocket and pull out my wallet, slipping the guy all the cash I have which is two hundred bucks. "That enough to keep you quiet and leave us alone for a bit?"

He takes it. "Confidentiality bought." He does a little bow and wanders off in his thong with his round butt cheeks wobbling with every step.

A scrunched-up napkin hits my head, and I turn back to Ollie.

"Why'd you make the pretty man disappear?"

I expect Lennon to not like that. Instead he agrees.

I throw my hands up in defeat, but Jet puts his hands around my shoulders.

"He did it because I'm the only one he needs."

"Exactly."

Jet pulls my head down to bring our mouths together hard and fierce.

I pull back before Jet can try to take it further and the guys get a different kind of show. "I think it's time we get back to our hotel."

"I'm totally loving your foresight to rent a hotel room and not stay with Matt and Noah."

Aww, poor Jet thinks he's getting some action when we get back, but I know him. I've seen him drunk countless times these last few months on the road, where he's been contractually obligated to go to the after-party and do the meet and greets with VIPs. Alcohol flows freely at those things. I can already see what's going to happen tonight. He'll probably fall asleep in the car on the way back and won't even stir when I carry him up to bed.

Then tomorrow will come, and he'll spring out of bed fresh as a fucking daisy with no sign of a hangover.

Rock stars are hard to keep up with, and mine certainly keeps me on my toes.

I can't wait for our forever to start.

CHAPTER TWENTY-FOUR

JET

The feel of my husband's hot, wet mouth moving over my needy and aching cock never gets old. Even now, *years* after we were married.

Our life together has been the craziest journey in the best possible way, and it's only about to get crazier. Or calmer. I really don't know how it's gonna go yet.

Soren's finger circles my hole and gently pushes in.

I throw my head back as I lie horizontally across the bed while he's on his knees on the floor. My ass inches closer to the edge of the mattress.

"I need you to fuck me," I breathe.

He pushes another finger in, and his mouth releases me with a wet pop. "We don't have time. We need to get off fast before we have to meet the others in the food hut for dinner."

I sigh because he's right. We're probably lucky they haven't come looking for us yet.

"Why did we agree to come on another group vacation?" I mumble.

Soren ignores me. He goes back to sucking me, while I smell the telltale scent of Fiji.

The real Fiji.

Coconut and sun mixed with cum—the way I always remember it.

We came back for our honeymoon six years ago but haven't had the chance to visit again.

Until now.

Soren relaxes his throat and takes me all the way in until his nose nuzzles my groin.

"Fuck, babe. I really need you to fuck me. You could slip it in. Like, right now."

His fingers press against my prostate, telling me his answer. *We have no time, and I'm going to drive you fucking wild.* Though his shoulders do shake as if he's trying to contain his laughter.

Now, that's talented. Laughing with a cock in your mouth.

My man's gag reflex needs, like, an award or something. Right now, I'm willing to offer up all my Grammys.

He rubs over the sensitive spot until I'm trembling and incoherent. He doesn't let up even for a second. Soren's on a mission to get me off as fast as possible, and I know it won't take much longer.

All it takes is his free hand reaching up toward my nipple. I don't even think he brushes over it before I'm convulsing and emptying into Soren's mouth.

He allows me no recovery time, but I can't complain. His body is still as hard and firm as it was when he played hockey, and when it starts climbing up me, I know we're not done.

I'm spent, but I can't wait to have my mouth on him.

Soren straddles my chest and grips his cock hard, guiding it to my mouth and running the tip along my lips.

A drop of precum leaks onto my chin, and I don't hesitate to lick it up, catching the underside of Soren's cock while I do it.

He releases a shuddery breath. "Open up."

My mouth opens wide.

"Suck only the tip," Soren orders, and I love it.

While I close my lips over his swollen head, Soren strokes his hard shaft.

He groans, and his hand moves faster until I feel the first spurts of his release on my tongue.

"Love you," he grunts.

Of course he does. I'm fucking awesome.

I swallow all of him, and then he flops onto the bed next to me.

We bask in the afterglow of orgasms, but it doesn't last long.

Soren turns his head toward me. "Are you ready to tell everyone?"

"Guess so. Still can't believe it's happening though."

My husband smiles. "Oh, it's happening." He stands and moves toward his suitcase to pull out the photo from a sonogram last week.

It's really happening.

"Guess I better get up. My muscles kinda don't want me to though. They're all … liquid-y."

"Up," Soren orders, and my dick thinks he's talking to it. Though it only twitches and then dies again. So not ready for another round yet.

We throw on clothes and make our way from the exact cabin we fell in love in years ago toward the food hut.

Surprisingly, we're the last ones to arrive. Only surprising because there are two other childless couples here, and I assumed they would be doing what we were.

But nope, there everyone is, the entire gay brigade plus a few stowaways. Seven-year-old Jackie is on her tablet with her headphones, not paying attention. Her baby brother, Noah Huntington the Fourth, is in Matt's lap chewing on something. He's teething, apparently. Yay, something to look forward to.

Talon and Miller's six- and five-year-old boys, Peyton and Brady, are chasing each other around the table fighting over which NFL team they're going to play for when they're older. I think Talon and Miller have learned to tune them out by now. They're eating normally as if they can't hear their kids who are loud as fuck.

I hope my baby comes with a mute button.

God, I'm so not ready to be a parent.

But when I turn to Soren and see the smile on his face as he watches our niece and nephews, I know he'll be enough for both of us.

I want this baby, but fuck … parenting? I'm not sure if I still qualify to look after myself even though I hit the big 3-0 this year.

I might not be ready, but Soren so is, and I promised him years ago, when he did the same to me, that we'd always give what the other needs.

We take our seats, and Soren squeezes my leg under the table.

Ooh, look, wine!

I pour myself a glass and down it while Soren chuckles.

It's not that I'm scared to tell everyone. They'll be ecstatic. It's the fact saying it out loud will make it real. Well, it's already real, but it'll make it *more real.*

Soren gives me a nod.

"Hey, guys?" I croak.

Everyone turns their attention to me.

"We, umm, need to tell y'all something?" I clear my throat.

Maybe the real reason I'm freaking out is because I worry they'll think the same way as me. That I'm not ready. That me being a *father* should be illegal. And there's no way these guys will hold back. It's *them.*

"The last time we were all here, it was because Noah was convinced it'd be his last time. His last hurrah. Their *final play.*" Little did they know they'd be back every single year.

It's the thing that I keep reiterating to myself when the idea of being a parent becomes too much. Noah was exactly the same as me going into the parenthood thing—convinced he would fuck it up. Convinced it would change his life for the worst ways instead of the best.

Seeing him over the years with his kids gives me all the faith in the world I can pull this off. Not only did Noah pull through, he could very well be the best parent I know in this room.

He once told me that he felt like he was failing. He didn't know if they chose the right school for Jackie, if they were giving her the right tools to be able to succeed in life. I still remember what I told him when he said, "What if I fail her?"

I looked him in the eyes and said, "The fact you care so much about failing her means you won't."

And as Soren slips the sonogram photo into my hand, I realize I'm going to be the same way with this child.

The reason I'm reluctant is because I'm worried I'll turn out like my parents—that I won't be good enough. That the kidlet deserves better.

Then I remind myself that I won't ever let that happen.

We haven't met the baby yet, but I'm already in love.

And these guys will understand that. They'll know all my reservations, and while that won't stop them from mocking me, it will make them help out if we need it.

This group has been through so much together. So many ups and downs. But the one thing we've all had these last ten years is each other.

My life with Soren might be about to change drastically, but the love we have for these guys and the support they give will never waver.

We're about to add another member to the gay brigade family.

I slide the photo onto the tabletop. Faces around the table light up and eyes widen.

"Guess this is our *final play*."

THE END

What am I supposed to do with my life now?

This series has been an amazing ride, and I'm sad that it's done. The series and these characters may be retired, but that doesn't necessarily mean this universe is finished ;)

AFTERWORD

THANK YOU - First and foremost, a BIG thank you to May Archer who lent me Silas and her town of O'Leary for Talon and Miller's wedding. (If you haven't read her Love in O'Leary series, you NEED to.)

And secondly, I want to thank every single person who has supported and loved this series. From my readers to my entire squad of betas, early readers, editors, cover designers, ARC readers, and PR team.

Join Absolutely Eden to keep up to date with Eden Finley news: https://www.facebook.com/groups/absolutelyeden/

Alternatively, you can join my mailing list: http://eepurl.com/bS1OFH

ALSO BY EDEN FINLEY

https://amzn.to/2zUlM16

https://www.edenfinley.com

FAKE BOYFRIEND SERIES

Fake Out

Trick Play

Deke

Blindsided

Hat Trick

Novellas:

Fake Boyfriend Breakaways: A Short Story Collection

Final Play

STEELE BROTHERS

Unwritten Law

Unspoken Vow

ROYAL OBLIGATION

Unprincely (M/M/F)

Made in the USA
Monee, IL
22 April 2023